Echoes From the Past

The War Elephant

a historical novel

John Chadwell

Text copyright © 2025 by John Chadwell
Cover and illustrations by John Chadwell with AI

All rights reserved.
No portion of this book may be used or reproduced
in any form or by any means without written permission from the
Publisher.

Library of Congress Cataloging-in-Publication Data
Chadwell, John, 1946-
979-8-9889084-6-3 (alk paper)
Library of Congress Control Number: 2025930458

Printed Page Press
Imprint of All About Kids Publishing
7680 Monterey St. #307
Gilroy, CA 95020
www.allaboutkidspub.com

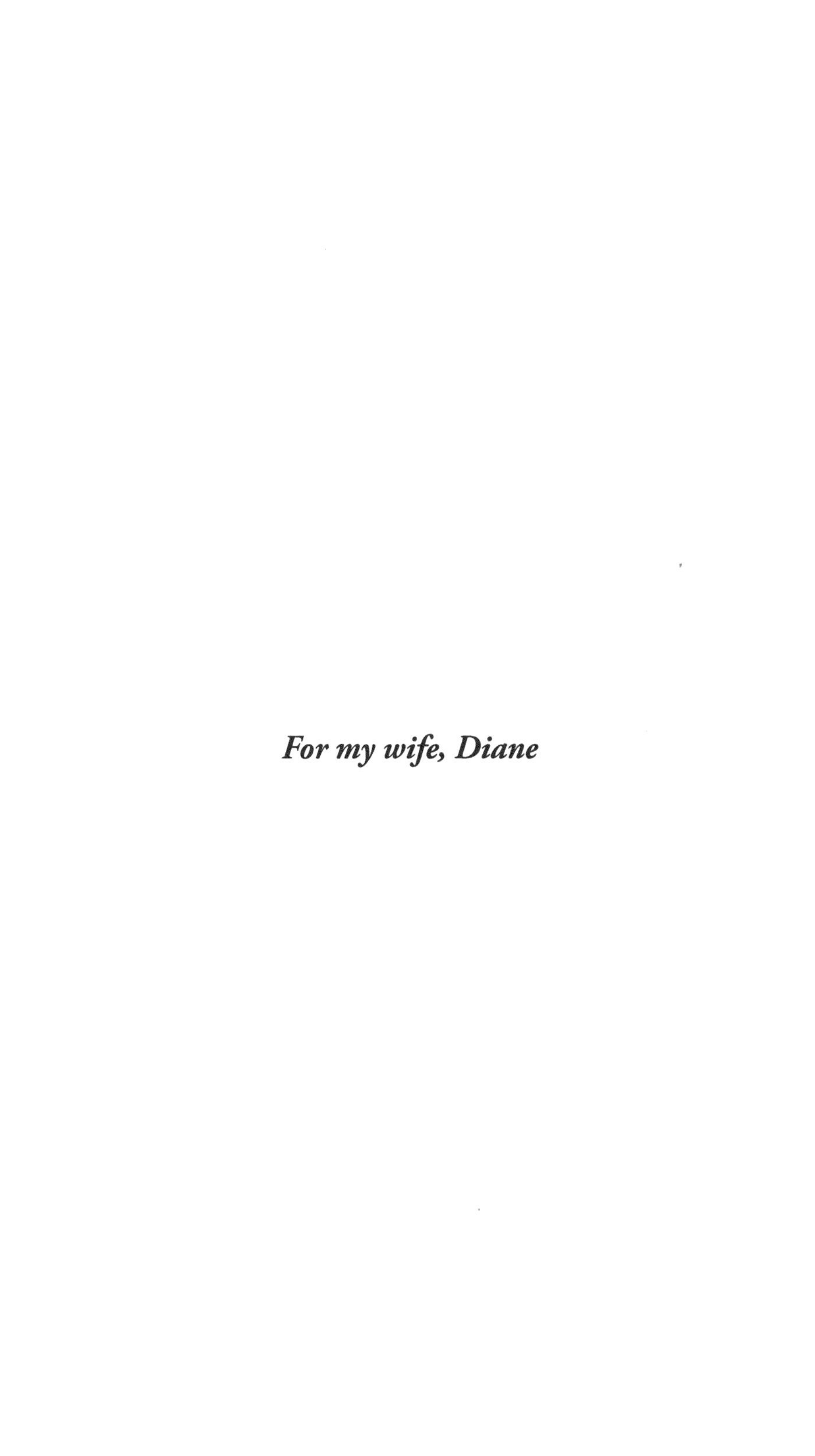

For my wife, Diane

Contents

Prologue

The years this story takes place are from 225 BC (Before Christ) to 201 BC. The years decrease because they are according to the Gregorian Calendar, which in 1850 AD replaced the Julian calendar (named for Julius Ceasar) that had been used since 49 BC. Today, the Gregorian calendar is used in most of the world. The years after the birth of Christ are followed by AD (Anno Domini, *In the year of the Lord).*

Interestingly, even though the Gregorian calendar would designate all years after Jesus' birth, Jesus would have been using the Julian calendar, or as it's often referred to as, the Roman calendar, which would have made the date of his birth at around 753, which is how many years had passed since the foundation of the Roman Republic.

From 1 BC going back in time using the Gregorian calendar, the years would increase. For instance, using the timeframe of our story, 225 BC to 201 BC, historical events around the Mediterranean region where the story unfolds prior to it included Alexander the Great conquering Egypt in 332 BC; the beginning of the war between Athens and Sparta in 431 BC; the Persian invasion of Greece, which was stopped by Sparta in 480 BC; the Persian king

Cyrus the Great conquered Babylon in 539 BC; the Assyrian king Sargon II conquered the Northern Kingdom of Israel in 721 BC. And it is believed that Moses led the Israelites out of Egypt around 3,500 BC.

Likewise, moving forward from 1 AD, the years increase to where we are today at the year 2025 AD, when this story was first published.

A sizable portion of our story takes place during what came to be called the Second Punic War (there were three separate Punic Wars) that took place between 218 BC and 202 BC. The original accounts of the three Punic Wars were written by several ancient historians, including Polybius, a Greek citizen whose work is considered one the most important sources of the Punic Wars. This war was led by Carthaginian political leader and General of the Army, Hannibal Barca, who crossed the Alps with over one hundred twenty thousand men, five thousand horses, and thirty-seven elephants.

The war began after the siege of Saguntum (the modern town of Sagunto, Spain), which was allied to Rome and located near Carthaginian territory in Hispania. Hannibal captured the city in 219 BC, violating a treaty between Rome and Carthage, after which Rome declared war on Carthage.

The core of Hannibal's army was around fifty-thousand infantrymen. They were composed of various units from Carthage and its territories, including Libyans, Spaniards, and Numidians. His cavalry was around twelve thousand Numidian horsemen, known for their speed, agility, and skill in mounted combat.

His war elephants were trained to charge into battle, trampling and scattering the enemy. While their impact was mostly psychological warfare, they inflicted hundreds if not thousands of Roman casualties. In one battle alone more than fifty-thousand Roman soldiers were killed by Carthaginian soldiers and elephants.

The war raged across multiple fronts. Hannibal dominated in Italia, while the Romans held their ground in Hispania and Sicily. It was a war of attrition, and while Rome could deploy hundreds of thousands of new recruits, Hannibal only had those who came across the Alps with him, and a few thousand Gaul allies, and his supply line was strung out through the Alps. Roman general Publius Cornelius Scipio, referred to as Scipio in historical accounts, for whom North Africa was eventually named, took the war to Carthage and defeated Hannibal's army at the Battle of Zama in 202 BC, ending the Second Punic War. The resulting Peace Treaty of Zama forced Carthage to surrender Hispania and its navy, and pay ten-thousand silver talents, which was equivalent to over three hundred tons of silver.

In our historical-fiction account of Hannibal's war against Rome, one of those thirty-seven elephants was a female named Surus, (based on an actual male elephant that took part in the war) was especially noteworthy in that she was a giant North African elephant accompanied by her handler or mahout, a fourteen-year-old autistic boy named Titus Aurelius, both of whom Hannibal adopted and protected during the war. The two had a bond uncommon between a human and animal unheard of in ancient times.

Chapter One

LEPCIS PARVA, CARTHAGE, THE YEAR 225 BC

Surus, which meant *The Syrian*, indicating where she possibly came from, was thirty-five years old when she first met Titus Aurelius, who was just seven. The boy was of Phoenician heritage, stemming from the Canaanites of the eastern Mediterranean region (present-day Lebanon, Israel, and Syria). He was of average height, slight build, olive skin, wavy brown hair, and gentle green eyes. Surus was big. Very big. Twice as large as her cousins in the herd of fifteen elephants. She was taller, heavier and her long, curved tusks were massive.

Carthaginian construction taskmasters had captured Surus when she was eight years old and took her from the forest, the only home she had ever known, as well as from her mother, aunts, and cousins. A freed Germanic slave was hired to domesticate, not tame, Surus and put her to work clearing trees to be used primarily for boat building, a highly prized skill passed down from Phoenician ancestors. The sturdy ships were used to wage war or conduct trade, depending on the political entanglements or mood for conquest at any given moment. Those used for war could be gigantic, some with citizen crews of up to seven thousand (more than a modern aircraft carrier has).

The Carthaginian Empire during the third century BC centered around the Colony of Carthage, founded by the Phoenician Queen Elissa from Tyre in 814 BC as a maritime rival to Rome. After Rome razed Carthage during the Third Punic War, 149-146 BC, it was eventually conquered by Arabs, and the area would be renamed Tunisia. For a time, though, Carthage controlled parts of North Africa, Hispania, and several Mediterranean islands.

The other players in this constant game of one-upmanship involved the Roman Republic, which controlled parts of Hispania and Sicily, and was constantly pushing the country's boundaries at the expense of its neighbors, including Hispania, the Ptolemaic Kingdom of Egypt, the Seleucid Empire, the Kingdom of Numidia, and the various Greek city-states.

Because of her uncommon size and superior strength, Surus had been used to haul heavy stones and logs carried on sleds to build a road from Lepcis Parva (modern Lampta, Tunisia) the wealthiest city in Carthage located along the eastern seaboard, where Titus's family lived, some ten thousand five hundred sixty Egyptian cubits (three miles) inland. Titus' father Lucius was tasked to repair the four-century-old temples dedicated to Baal Hammon, the chief god of Carthage, and his consort, Tanit, the goddess of life, fertility, and war, which had been damaged by earthquakes.

Lucius, a highly admired master builder and tradesman, won the contract, more through bribes than skill, from Hamilcar Barca, the Carthaginian general and statesman, whose guerrilla warfare skills had expanded Carthage's territory into Hispania during the First Punic War that included the establishment of New Carthage (modern-day Cartegena) along with what is now the Spanish coast.

If there could be such a thing as love between a human and an elephant, such was the case for Titus and Surus. Remarkably, Surus had remained passive despite having been treated, through kicks and prodding with hooks called ankuses. She could out-pull or lift more weight than any two elephants. Despite her obvious value, she was often left unattended and alone at night, chained to a tree, sometimes without sufficient food and water.

By the standards of the time, her successions of mahouts or handlers were not considered overly cruel. They just did not consider her anything more important than any other tool, and if they could coax or bully her to work, they gave her happiness no thought.

The day Lucius bought Surus and told Titus he would be responsible for her future training and care, everything changed for her.

Lucius instinctively knew Surus was an exceptional animal who had been sorely mistreated. He knew his son needed to take on responsibility to learn a trade and contribute to the family's wealth. He also knew Titus was kind and, as his only son, needed the companionship of this gentle giant.

Chapter Two

It was no secret in the village that Titus was different from the other children (it would be more than twenty-one hundred years before his behavior was understood for what it was after a psychiatrist called it *early infantile autism* to describe impaired social and language skills, repetitive behaviors, and resistance to change).

Lucius loved his only son from the day of his birth and for the first two years the boy acted like any other child: he was happy all the time; he smiled and cooed at his parents and began crawling at nine months. He was walking at a year and gleefully chasing his two sisters and cousins. At eighteen months he said his first word. To his father's joy the boy's first word was *papa*. Then, just before his second birthday, everything changed.

His sisters noticed it first. It was as if he forgot how to play or talk. He started to wander away from the other children and no longer responded to his name. His bright eyes dulled, and he would not look at anyone as his head began to rock back and forth. Suddenly, he was mute and indifferent to his family and any other human. Then he became aggressive, especially to his father.

By his fifth birthday his entire personality changed again. He could communicate with gestures and his attention began to focus on the animals around the village. He would make pets of animals when there was no concept of pets in ancient times. If an animal were sick or injured, he intuitively knew a treatment or cure.

Then he began to notice the elephants. His father feared the boy might be injured if he were to venture too close to the elephants, but Titus gravitated toward them at every opportunity. The animals knew there was something different about Titus and they would surprise the people by going up to him for no apparent reason other than to receive his touch.

It did not matter that the other children teased him. He did not seem to notice or respond to the taunts. Adults wondered if he was demon-possessed because of his erratic behavior that included sudden nonsensical outbursts. Because of his odd behavior in not looking at people, speaking little, and when he did, he would often repeat words in a sing-song way, one of the priests at the Baal Hammon temple tried to convince Lucius to give the boy up as a sacrifice.

As a trader, Lucius traveled extensively throughout the Mediterranean nations, including the Judah and Israel regions of the powerful Assyrian and Babylonian Kingdoms.

Lucius was wealthy and powerful. He was able to use a well-placed bribe of gold bracelets he bought from a local band of Hebrews who claimed to be the remnants of the Tribe of Benjamin, from the region of the same name after one of the twelve sons of Jacob, also called Israel, the son of Isaac and Rebecca.

Rebuffed, the priest moved on to a poor family that had more children than they could feed. With a promise of a blessing from Baal Hammon on their next crop, they gave up their youngest girl to be sacrificed on the burning altar.

Despite Titus' strangeness, Lucius' love for the boy never wavered and he sought moral authority to keep him from giving his son up for sacrifice. He found such support when he began trading with the Hebrews, who were tinkerers that dealt in gold and silver jewelry, as well as bronze and iron weapons. In particular, he was interested in obtaining the fine Damascus Steel swords and spears the Hebrews bought from the blacksmiths in the City of Syria, the capital of the Roman province, also called Syria.

Over the years of trading, when he often took Titus with him, the Hebrews told Lucius about their strange god they called Adonai, which they told him meant *The Name*, because they were forbidden to speak their god's actual name, *Yahweh*.

This new god appealed to Lucius because the Hebrews told him that while *Yahweh* was a jealous god, he had only once demanded the sacrifice of a child called Isaac but had changed his mind when the father, Abraham, willingly offered his son up. The Hebrews showed Lucius scrolls made of parchment sheets of kosher animal skins sewn together they called the *Torah* and written in Tiberian Hebrew that they taught him to read.

In particular, besides the book called Genesis, he enjoyed the one called Exodus that told how the Hebrew god had taken their ancestors out of Egypt after more than four hundred years of slavery and how he often tested his chosen people, and even though they constantly failed to measure up he still forgave them.

Lucius liked the idea of a god who would forgive a man's sins because he was the worst sinner he knew, and he feared for his soul, now that he believed he might have one. While he did not give a thought to converting, Lucius adopted those attributes of the Hebrew god that appealed to him, while not neglecting to also pray to Baal Hammon for continued good fortune with his crops and trading ventures.

The day Surus met Titus not only changed her life but her opinion of humans, at least of this one human child.

Lucius brought the boy to the elephant as she stood chained to a tree apart from the other unrelated elephants, with whom she had never bonded. She looked down at Titus suspiciously because her eyesight was not as keen as were her olfactory senses that detected food, water, and danger.

Her massive head swayed back and forth and a low, rumbling sound, resembling the purr of a large cat, emanated from her throat, communicating her curiosity about the little human.

Her trunk hung listlessly, but the tip or proboscis began to twitch slightly at the boy's strange scent. Other humans smelled earthy, even foul to her, while the boy smelled almost sweet, like green grass with the morning dew still on it. She lifted her trunk to lightly touch his cheek and inhaled the essence of him.

She had never known a human like Titus who was singularly

attentive to animals as well as his own hygiene. She would come to know the boy took no fewer than three baths a day, and from this day forward she would accompany him to the river for daily scrub downs and gentle touches that would strengthen the bond between them unknown to animals of the ancient world where they were used for food, clothing, labor, or sacrifice, but seldom appreciated as sentient beings.

She gazed at Titus as his father held the boy's hand out to touch her. His head remained bowed, and he would not look up at her. His hand remained motionless as it pressed against her trunk. Then, ever so slowly, his fingers began to stroke and explore her wrinkled skin.

At first, the boy's demeanor mirrored the elephant's listless behavior. Slowly, though, Titus raised his head, and his dull expression changed to one of fascination as he looked up into her magnificent brown eyes, shielded by long, curly lashes. Lucius marveled at his son's behavior as it changed before his eyes. He could not recall the boy interacting with humans in such a manner.

The elephant looked down at the boy. She blinked: He smiled.

Chapter Three

That was the first time Lucius had seen Titus smile since he was two. He was further stunned when his son spoke a single word—in Hebrew, "Hesed."

"How does he know this word," Lucius marveled because he knew from his lessons with the rabbi of the Hebrew tribe that *hesed* had many meanings, including love, kindness, and devotion, but all were meant as appropriate behavior for relationships or covenants between humans, or humans and their god. *Does my son believe Surus to be a god*, Lucius wondered.

Upon meeting the gentle female elephant, the boy was initially reserved and cautious. His non-communicative tendencies began to shift in response to her calming presence and imperceptible throaty rumblings. As the two beings shared moments of quiet observation and mutual curiosity, a subtle transformation took place. The boy's non-verbal cues evolved, with increased eye contact and the emergence of subtle smiles showing the newfound connection. The rhythmic movements of the elephant and the soothing sounds she made served as a non-threatening sensory experience for the boy, creating a bridge for communication beyond words.

Over the next three years, this unique bond grew between the two, characterized by a shared understanding that transcended conventional communication. Titus found comfort in the consistent and gentle nature of the elephant, leading to a gradual reduction in self-isolating behaviors. Through this connection, he discovered a source of solace and companionship, fostering a positive impact on his overall well-being.

From the first time Titus and Surus ventured to the river together everyone in the village gawked at them in disbelief, fear, and wonder. Gone were the chains and hooks to control the beast as the strange boy led the elephant to the water with his left hand resting on her right tusk. The people noticed how the elephant gently touched the boy's head with her trunk, tousling his hair and rubbing his shoulders, sometimes even playfully encircling his neck as she pulled him to her so their heads would touch. They also noticed that Titus was constantly smiling and even seemed to be talking to the elephant. No one had ever heard him say a single word and they were mesmerized at the change.

By the fourth year the villagers had become accustomed to seeing them together. Surus was known even beyond the village as the strongest, most capable elephant at hauling massive loads, and being fiercely protective of Titus, and by extension, his family. She would follow him through the village markets, easing through aisles of goods and foodstuff barely causing a scene as people would reach out to touch her, no longer concerned that she might cause problems.

That changed on the day a rogue bull elephant stampeded into the village in a blind rage and began tearing through homes and trampling anyone unfortunate enough to be in its path. The bull crushed a man who thrust a spear at it to protect his children as they ran away screaming in terror. It billowed angrily and plunged through several buildings, ripping them apart with his trunk and tusks.

Titus and Surus were at the center of the village when they heard the panicked screams of the villagers and the trumpeting call of the killer elephant. Titus scrambled up Surus' trunk, straddled her neck, and urged her to hurry toward the screams. At first, the people believed there were two elephants wreaking havoc on the village. But it quickly became clear this elephant was on a mission to save them.

Surus slid to a stop in a clearing where several huts had been trampled flat. The bull's back was to her, but he sensed her presence and spun around to face her. The bull raised its trunk and gave a throaty challenge as he shook his head side to side creating a cloud of dust.

Except for protecting a calf, it would be rare for a cow elephant to challenge a bull. Since she had never born a calf, the villagers had become her extended family, and she would protect them at all costs. Surus raised her trunk to answer the challenge and to catch the bull's scent.

Though it had been over twenty years since her capture and being separated from the herd, she remembered the scent of this male. She also remembered her mother, as the matriarch, had driven the young bull from the herd when he began to challenge her dominance.

Surus hesitated.

The bull charged, catching her by surprise. He crashed into her, violently knocking her off balance. For only a moment she seemed unsure of how to react, but when she saw Titus had been thrown off her back into the path of the angry bull, she did not hesitate. Titus scrambled to his feet, shaken. He turned to face the bull as it towered over him and pulled off the long sling he kept wrapped around his shoulders. The bull lowered its head, intent on crushing him.

This time, the bull was surprised not only that a cow elephant would challenge him but would do so to save a human. He was only slightly smaller than Surus but in her devotion to the boy she would fight him to the death. She bellowed and rammed her head into the bull's side pushing him back toward the forest.

The clash of ivory tusks echoed through the village as the two elephants engaged in a fierce struggle. Houses trembled as the ground quivered beneath their colossal weight. Terrified villagers sought refuge in their homes, peering cautiously from behind windows and doors.

Surus, despite her size, displayed remarkable agility as she skillfully evaded the bull's relentless attacks. Her eyes reflected determination, fueled not by aggression but by a deep sense of responsibility toward humans.

The battle raged on, and the once peaceful village was transformed into a battleground of huge proportions. Mud and dust filled the air as the elephants continued their struggle, oblivious to the destruction they left in their wake. Wooden structures crumbled like ancient ruins beneath the colossal strength of the warring giants.

Titus dodged the battling titans. He dipped his fingers into the pouch on his belt and took out two round stones, slipped one in the sling. As the bull began another charge, he let fly the stone that struck the animal in its left eye, causing it to stop the charge, shaking his head in anger and pain. The boy slipped the second stone in the sling as the bull charged at him. Surus saw the bull's intent to harm her human, bellowed a growling scream and charged the bull, ramming him in the side, impaling him with her left tusk. The bull raged in anger and pulled free of her. Titus flung the second stone that careened off the bull's skull.

Inside the village the magistrate, a wise and elderly man named Harish, recognized that drastic measures were needed to protect his people. He hurriedly gathered the villagers and devised a plan to distract the bull, allowing Surus an opportunity to end the conflict.

Villagers armed with flaming torches and loud drums approached from the sides, diverting the bull's attention momentarily. Surus seized the opportunity and communicated with a series of low-frequency rumbles that echoed through the air. The bull elephant hesitated, caught between his fury and the undeniable calm exuded by Surus.

In a moment of stillness, the villagers hoped for a resolution. However, the bull, unwilling to yield, charged once more, forcing Surus to move between it and the villagers. With a powerful thrust of her tusks, she redirected the bull's attack away from the village back into the forest. Only Titus was brave and loyal enough to follow them into the darkness.

The two elephants crashed through the surrounding foliage, leaving a trail of destruction in their wake. Surus' determination to protect the villagers remained unwavering, but she knew that the only way to ensure their safety was to subdue the aggressive bull, by lethal means, if need be.

The duel reached its climax deep in the forest, out of sight of the villagers. Drawing on her strength and intelligence, she countered the bull's every move. The battle was intense, the night filled with the sounds of trumpeting and crashing trees.

In a decisive moment, Surus used her sheer mass to pin the bull to the ground. Exhausted and defeated, the bull bellowed in frustration. Surus, her eyes reflecting sadness and resolution, raised her tusks high to deliver a swift, fatal blow. But then she stopped the attack and stepped away from the exhausted bull.

As Titus stood beside her with his hand on her front leg, they watched as the bull struggled to his feet, gave them one last glance, turned, and disappeared in the depths of the forest. They never would know if he died or simply chose not to return.

Even though victorious, Surus bore the weight of the conflict in her heart. Much of the once vibrant village lay in ruins, a testament to the cost of defending the lives of those she had instinctually sworn to protect.

As the dawn broke, Surus stood amidst the remnants of the village she had fought so fiercely to safeguard. The sun's rays bathed her in a gentle glow, revealing the scars of battle etched on her torn, blood-stained skin. With Titus at her side, she had become a fearful guardian, a symbol of sacrifice and unwavering courage in the face of adversity.

Chapter Four

"Titus, my son, I want to talk to you about what happened last night. Can we speak of it?" Lucius said to his son while they sat on the riverbank watching Surus as she took long drafts of water in her trunk and sprayed it over her body, washing away the dirt and blood from the terrible fight.

Titus had become more communicative with his father over the last few months because of his calming interaction with the elephant, though he still found it difficult to look into his father's eyes. "Can we talk about what happened?" Lucius urged.

"Yes," Titus answered.

Lucius had grown accustomed to his son's monosyllabic answers and knew he sometimes had to walk his son through a conversation, one question or comment at a time.

"You know, I am very proud of you and Surus." Titus nodded, staring at his hands.

"You did a brave and noble thing by standing up to that elephant. He was a danger to our village and our crops. You saved many lives."

"Surus saved the village. I helped, a little," Titus answered in a flat, monotone whisper, then repeated, "Surus did. I helped. A little."

"More than a little, my son. You trained Surus to be loyal. She was protecting her family."

"He wanted to hurt us," Titus said of the bull elephant.

"Yes, he did."

"Why?"

"I do not know. Perhaps someone hurt him, and he hated all people," Lucius said, adding as he touched Titus' head. The boy started to shrink away from the touch as he did when he was younger, but now he allowed his father to do so. "You did not run away and stayed with Surus to protect her with your sling. You caused the bull to be distracted and gave Surus the chance she needed to defeat him. You were smart and courageous."

"She listens to me. I listen to her," Titus said. "I listen. We understand each other. We are family. Yes, family."

Lucius smiled at his son. "You and your elephant are a family. And she is also part of our family. We love you and we are proud of you. You are a special boy. You have a gift. You can communicate with animals in a way that no one else can. You can see things that others cannot. You can learn things that others cannot. You are different, but you are not less. You are more."

"Sometimes I feel I do not belong," Titus said. "Others do not understand me."

"I know it is hard. People fear what they do not understand. They judge what they do not know. But you must not be bothered by them. Remember that you are not alone. You have your elephant. You have your mother and me, and your sisters."

Chapter Five

By the time he was thirteen, Titus was already considered a man in his society. He had grown into a strong young man with a kind heart and a wild spirit of almost mythical proportions because of his relationship with Surus. They had fought together to defeat the rogue killer elephant and saved the people of Lepcis Parva.

After the battle they returned to their lives of toiling in the woodlands as if nothing had happened. They worked as a well-honed team. He rode atop Surus, coaxing her with gentle tickles with his toes behind her ears and clicks of his tongue, transcending any need for words, which was fine with him because he still had difficulty speaking his thoughts without having to think about each word before uttering it. In the quietude of the dark forests, their silent communication echoed louder than a gentle breeze whispering through the timbers.

Her strength matched the ancient trees they transported together. In the vast woodlands their connection grew deeper each day, transcending the bounds of master and beast of burden. They worked in tandem, their bond strengthening like the fibers of the ropes they used to drag the fallen giants from the forest.

Word of Titus' and Surus' remarkable partnership spread throughout Carthage, reaching neighboring villages and catching the attention of those who sought strength and bravery beyond the realms of forestry.

Always up for a reason for a festival, the people were eager for any reason to come together with other villages to celebrate with tasty food, family and friends, and games to cheer on the competitors, and to gamble. It was the time of the Summer Solstice, the longest day of the year, and reason enough to celebrate.

There were numerous endurance competitions. In the tradition of the Greek Olympics young men wrestled, ran the marathon, and competed with javelins, discus, bow and arrows, spears, horse races, and the newest event, the elephant pull.

Whispers of the unbeatable duo of Titus and Surus had reached the ears of organizers seeking participants from far and wide. Ten elephants, their mahouts, and their financial backers came to challenge the local heroes.

Little did they know that their triumphs would attract more than just accolades. Hasdrubal, one of the two younger brothers of Hannibal Barca, son of Hamilcar, came to the village. He was always in search of extraordinary talents and had heard the fantastic tales of the formidable pair. Drawn by the prospect of an elephant with unparalleled strength and a young man with an unwavering spirit, Hasdrubal arrived in Lepcis Parva as the games were about to begin.

In the heart of the competition arena, surrounded by towers with hundreds of onlookers, most of whom were ready to place wagers on their favorites, Titus and Surus showcased their unparalleled synchronization. The ground trembled beneath Surus' mighty steps as they outperformed their competitors in log pulls and maze running, earning admiration, respect, and gold. Lepcis Parva, once a humble fishing and trading village that had grown into an important seaport, now basked in the glory brought by Titus' and Surus' victories.

In a tug-of-war competition Surus had made short shift of every elephant put up against her. The organizers and the crowd grew impatient to see her take on more challenges and it was first decided to match her against two other elephants harnessed in tandem.

When she handily dragged them backwards across the clearing, Lucius bragged that Surus could best three grown elephants. By that time, he had consumed more wine than he was accustomed to, which compelled him to believe nothing was beyond Titus' and Surus' abilities.

Titus looked at his father skeptically when he proposed the match. He looked up into Surus' expressive eyes and from what he could tell she was in a playful mood and was willing to do whatever he asked of her. He nodded in acquiesce to Lucius, who grinned and shouted to the crowd, "They agree to the match."

A third elephant was brought up and quickly harnessed to the long rope stretched across the clearing to bound the four elephants together. Their three mahouts looked across the field at the monstrous female elephant they had heard so much about. *Surely*, they thought, *she would not be able to best three elephants.* They certainly hoped not because each had wagered all they possessed on the outcome.

Surus stood poised, ready for Titus' signal. The visiting crowd was beginning to cheer for their favorites. The locals were eager to take all bets. They had seen Surus at her best and worst and had no doubt she would win.

The competition organizer or hellanodikai, a term borrowed from the Greeks, who was responsible for ensuring the rules of the games were followed, waved the flag and the audience cheered wildly.

Each of the three mahouts scampered up on their animal's backs and looked back at Surus and Titus as she lifted him up with her trunk. He settled in behind her ears, cooing to her and rubbing them. If she could smile, she would have been grinning ear to ear. She only gave her low rumble meant for Titus only.

As the flag dropped and Titus nudged her, Surus let out a mighty trumpeting roar, as her muscles rippling beneath her thick hide, she lunged forward, catching her three opponents by surprise. They strained against the ropes, their tusks scraping against the ground. But Surus, drawing upon her immense strength, stood her ground, her legs planted firmly like pillars of stone.

Titus leaned over and whispered a soothing song to her, his voice encouraging her. Surus, fueled by Titus's words, surged forward, her powerful legs propelling her body with astonishing force as the leather harness pulled tight around her chest. The ground trembled beneath her feet as she inched the other elephants closer and closer to the center line.

Surus' innate intelligence gave her a real sense of strategy and she knew brute force alone would not suffice. Her tusks, polished smooth from years of hauling timber and rocks, gleamed with a hint of mischief. Her ears, like vast silken banners, flapped rhythmically.

The thick ropes leading from the leather harnesses of all four elephants strained between them. The ground groaned under the collective effort of the four mountains of muscle. Surus leaned forward, her powerful hind legs churned up the earth. The other elephants, even though younger and eager, strained against the rope, their trumpeting calls echoing through the valley. The crowd went wild, screaming and cheering madly.

Suddenly, Surus stood motionless. With their combined power the three elephants could not make her budge. Titus looked over his shoulder at the three competitors. Patience was their weapon. As the others began to tire, pulling with blind fervor, he saw their chance and sang out, "Now, Surus. Now!"

Surus leaned into the harness and took a single step, then another. Her rear feet pushed forward with all her might. The three elephants were powerless against her as she slowly began to drag them backwards. They trumpeted angrily as their mahouts prodded them with their hooks. They tried, to no avail, to synchronize their powerful muscles to thwart Surus and Titus.

The end came suddenly. Surus continued to churn up dirt as she dug in with her hind legs and pushed forward with her front legs. One elephant toppled over backwards, nearly crushing its mahout. It screamed in panic and the man tumbled way from it. The other two lost all coordination and were quickly pulled off balance. No matter how hard one of the men tried to force his elephant forward the animal knew it had already been lost and began to back up voluntarily and was pulled across the line accompanied by the wild cheering of the crowd.

The elephant that had fallen struggled to its feet. It had not crossed the line. It gazed at Surus, challenging her. Surus met the challenge with a playful wiggle of her trunk, a silent taunt. The young elephant, a bull that had not yet grown wise with age, changed the rules of the game, and charged at Surus, his trunk raised like a battering ram.

With a single word from Titus, Surus sidestepped with the grace of a dancer, letting his momentum carry him past her. Then, with a swiftness that belied her size, she swung her front left leg, tripping him. He crumpled to the ground with a surprised yelp in a major face plant, his tusks clattering against the earth.

The third elephant was older than his two compatriots. He looked back at Surus. It seemed determined to take on Surus single-handed. This was a battle of wills, not brute force. They locked their eyes, their trunks mirroring each other in a silent duel. Surus knew this one would not be fooled by tricks. He was a veteran, like her. He respected her strength, her cunning.

Titus nudged behind Surus' ears. They leaned into the rope, muscles straining. The earth groaned; the rope sang a taut melody. They were locked in a dance of power, respect woven into every movement. Finally, with a slow, inexorable pull, Surus felt the tide turning. The elder started to give way. Inch by inch. No matter how hard the elder's handler beat on him to pull he knew he had been bested and lowered his head in silent submission.

Surus and Titus let out simultaneous triumphant trumpeting calls, a victory cry that echoed through the valley. It was not just about winning; it was about proving that even the wisest, the most experienced, could be outmaneuvered. Together, they had bested them not just with strength, but with cleverness. She was Surus, the mighty, the strategist, the undisputed champion of the elephantine tug-of-war. He was Titus, her companion, her protector, her champion.

As the crowd dispersed the other elephants shook the dust from their heads, offering playful nudges of respect. Titus knew their legend would grow. The tale of the warrior Titus and the mighty Surus, the elephant who could outsmart and outmaneuver even the strongest, would be whispered about around watering holes and under starlit skies, a testament to their cunning and enduring legacy.

Titus cheered and wrapped his arms across her broad neck.

"You did it, girl!" he exclaimed, his voice filled with emotion. "You are the strongest elephant in the world!"

Surus, her eyes twinkling with pride, touched his face with her trunk and let out a gentle trumpet, her breath tickling Titus's face. The bond between the elephant and her human was unbreakable, a testament to their trust and mutual respect.

Titus and Surus stood side by side, alone in the field, their silhouettes etched against the setting sun. Surus, the mighty elephant, had once again proven her dominance, but it was Titus' unwavering support that had fueled her victory. Together, they had conquered the arena, their partnership a symbol of strength, courage, and unwavering determination.

After witnessing the unbelievable performance, Hasdrubal sought Lucius as the legal owner of the elephant. He spoke of Hannibal's grand vision, of conquests and battles against Carthage's arch enemy, Rome, where their unique talents would be invaluable. Lucius, torn between the safety of his son and the allure of a greater purpose, faced an impossible choice. He stood at the crossroads of a life-altering decision. The air crackled with tension as the fate of Titus and Surus hung in the balance.

Hasdrubal, recognizing the hesitation, spoke passionately of the adventures that awaited Titus and Surus. The call of destiny resonated in his words, tempting Lucius to consider a path that transcended the familiar boundaries of their woodland existence. Yet, the father's love for his son clashed with the uncertainty of a future enshrouded in the fog of war.

In the end, it was Titus who spoke, his voice carrying the wisdom of the woods and the courage of youth. He expressed a desire to embark on this uncharted journey, to test the strength of their bond against challenges that reached beyond the horizon. Lucius, though reluctant, saw the fire in his son's eyes and nodded, granting his blessing.

Chapter Six

The Carthaginian sun beat down mercilessly, turning the dusty training ground into a shimmering furnace. Sweat stung Titus' eyes as he gripped the ankus, urging Surus forward. Draped in a canvas of war paint and leather armor, she lumbered through the obstacle course, her thick hide creased with exertion.

Titus felt his own muscles scream in protest. Yet, they pushed on. Their bond strengthened even more because of the unforgiving embrace of Hannibal's training camp.

Titus and Surus were an anomaly in the camp – a mere boy and his elephant, defying the norms of war with an unspoken language of clicks of the tongue and nudges with his toes. Their training was brutal. Days bled into weeks, filled with the clang of swords on shields, the guttural roars of war cries, and the ever-present threat of Hannibal's piercing gaze. Titus learned to read Surus' every twitch, every rumble in her throat and trunk. He learned to be an extension of her will, guiding her through intricate formations, his demeanor a calm counterpoint to the cacophony around them.

One blistering afternoon, during a mock battle, doubt gnawed at Titus as he stood beside Surus with a shield and spear on his back and his sling and pouch full of smooth, round stones. Carthaginians dressed as Roman legionaries, clad in crimson cloaks and wielding wooden swords, charged towards them. Fear, a cold serpent, coiled in his gut. What if Surus faltered? What if their bond, their fragile shield, shattered under the onslaught?

He saw it in Surus' eyes too, a flicker of uncertainty. The battlefield, usually a playground for their synchronized dance, suddenly seemed vast and terrifying. But then, something shifted. Surus' trunk, prehensile and strong, reached out and wrapped around Titus's arm, a silent reassurance. It was a touch not of fear, but of trust, of shared vulnerability.

With a guttural roar that shook the very ground, Surus charged. Titus, his fear melting into a fierce determination, ran beside her and urged her on. They became a whirlwind of dust and fury, Surus' tusks ripping through shields, her trunk sending men flying like rag dolls. The mock attack was all too real as men limped and ran out of her path. Titus, a tiny figure running in and out of her long legs used his sling to bring men much more powerful than him down.

That day, something changed in the camp. The seasoned warriors, who had scoffed at the boy and his elephant, now looked at them with grudging respect. Hannibal, his face a mask carved from stone, gave Titus the barest hint of a nod as he rode by on his tall, piercing black Arabian stallion.

It is enough, Titus thought.

Their legend grew. They were Hannibal's chosen.

They were more than just boy and beast; they were a single, unstoppable force, a living embodiment of Hannibal's audacious plan to crush Rome with the mighty army and his war elephants.

Chapter Seven

Ever since the end of the First Punic War twenty-four years before in 241 BC, Hamilcar Barca, and then his sons, Hannibal, Hasdrubal, and Mago plotted their revenge against Rome. What would become known to future generations and historians as the Second Punic War would establish Hannibal in the annals of history as the most courageous warrior and astute military tactician of all time.

Hamilcar would not live to see his revenge carried out. He died in 228 BC while fighting in Hispania yet again. While attempting to besiege a place called Helice his army was routed by the Celtiberian army and as he was attempting to escape by crossing the Jucar River he was thrown from his horse and drowned.

As part of his plan to take the fight to Rome, Hannibal wanted to use war elephants. This was not a new military tactic, by far. Elephants had been used in war and commerce over the prior two thousand years. Indian elephants played key roles in warfare, particularly by Macedonian king Alexander the Great during the Hellenistic Wars and the Battle of Hydaspes in 326 BC. In 264 BC Spartan general Xanthippus deployed one hundred elephants during fighting against Rome in Sicily. Hannibal inherited his African war elephants from his father who used them during the First Punic War, fought in Hispania. There were twenty surviving Indian elephants still in New Carthage on the Hispania coast.

Seventeen new recruits, including Surus, had been procured that would have to be transported by ship across the Mediterranean, a journey of at least a week at sea that would also involve transporting thousands of men and horses, six hundred oxen and cattle, two hundred mules, sheep and goats, and of course the seventeen African elephants. The army also had to take along hundreds of wagons, food for men and animals, weapons of every sort, and countless pieces of equipment, from camping gear and forges for the blacksmiths to cold-weather clothing. And then there were the camp followers comprised of craftsmen of every stripe, families of married men, slaves, and women who followed every campaign to earn money.

Since Titus and Surus came to Hannibal's camp the training never stopped. They joined the other elephants and their mahouts to learn how to march, charge, and fight. Surus was fitted for armor, made of thick leather and padding that protected her head, chest, and sides. She also wore bronze caps on her tusks, and sometimes a wooden platform on her back, where soldiers could stand and shoot arrows, throw spears, or hurl stones with slings.

Riding on Surus' neck, Titus learned how to use these weapons, but he still preferred to run beside her and use his sling to hit the enemy at a distance rather than to risk hand-to-hand combat with the more experienced Romans. When walking with her he also learned how to use the sword and shield while using her bulk and deadly tusks as added protection.

Titus and Surus also bonded with the other elephants and their mahouts, who became their friends and comrades. They shared stories, jokes, and songs around the campfires at night, and dreamed of glory and victory in the morning. Titus was proud to be part of this elite force, and he hoped to make his father and his country proud too.

But he also had doubts and fears. He wondered what would happen when they faced the Romans, who were known for their discipline, courage, adaptability, and ferocity. He wondered how Surus would react to the noise, the blood, and the pain. He wondered if they would survive, or if they would die together in a foreign land. He also wondered if war was worth it, or if there was a better way to settle differences.

He tried to push these thoughts away and focus on the present. He tried to enjoy the time he had with Surus, who was always there for him, no matter what. He wanted to remember that his father and the soldiers told him they were fighting for a noble cause. Most of all he hoped that he would be brave when the time came. He wanted to trust fate, even though he had little understanding of what fate was.

He did not know what the future would hold, but he knew one thing for sure: he and Surus would never give up, and they would never be apart. They were a team, and they were ready for war.

Chapter Eight

The year 219 BC found Titus and Surus still training daily for war at one of Hannibal's many camps on his vast properties outside Lepcis Parva. At thirteen, Titus was legally an adult under Carthaginian law, which meant he was free to do anything any adult male could do in the ancient world. As a citizen of Carthage, he could work for wages, own property, serve on councils, and even marry.

The highest honor for any Carthaginian male citizen, though, was to serve in its military, particularly aboard its warships, which were representative of their Phoenician ancestors who ruled the Mediterranean for over a century with their advanced ship designs and sheer numbers: Rome had hundreds of ships: Carthage had thousands.

None of these citizens' rights interested Titus. As he had been intently focused on animals only a few years before, he was now consumed with training for war. The concept of war eluded him. It was still a vague concept, but the challenge of practicing with the weapons of war, which included Surus, gave him the narrow focus suited for his intellectual capacity and had diminished much of the mental fog he had experienced as a child.

All the training also honed his body, and though only thirteen he was six feet tall and powerfully built. He was also fleet of foot and highly skilled at wrestling, which Hasdrubal had introduced him to. In this world wrestling was not just sport, it was a prelude to hand-to-hand combat. He was becoming a Carthaginian athlete-warrior in the classic sense of the mythical Greek warriors Achilles, the greatest warrior of the Trojan War; King Theseus, who killed the mythical Minotaur and united the Greek city-states; and Odysseus, king of Ithaca who designed the Trojan Horse.

On this day, Surus was learning how to smash through the bramble barriers filled with long thorns simulating those the Romans used as temporary fortifications around their mobile encampments. The thick leather armor and padding on her sides deflected the thorns as it would hopefully do against the Roman arrows and spears. At first, she was ill at ease with the armor, but she quickly grew used to it and did not protest as the men who designed it fitted on her each day.

And since the entire army would be sailing to Hispania, special mock-ups of gangways to barges floating in the river were used to acquaint the horses and elephants with the nautical aspect of war. Surus had always loved the water and had no apprehension about walking along a wooden gangway to a barge. When it was cast out into the rushing current and the barge began to rock violently, she quickly learned to steady herself, while resting her trunk on Titus' shoulders for comfort.

There were other elephants also training but Surus' immense size, loud trumpeting and fearless charges sent shivers down the spines of the other mahouts. The one aspect of their training that was most difficult for them at first was coordinating charges while surrounded by hundreds of Numidian calvary their horses and the shouting infantry as they beat their shields with their swords and spears.

Surus had never been around horses, and she seemed skittish when surrounded by them and their riders. But with patience and encouragement from Titus she quickly became at ease around them as they charged at mock fortifications.

Titus was curious about the horses and the men who rode them. He soon became friends with two young brothers, Micipsa and Gaia, the sons of King Marsinissa of Numidia, after they approached him one night out of curiosity about Surus. They had never seen an elephant and wanted to touch this most amazing animal. Titus wondered where they came from, and the nature of the magnificent animals they rode.

The brothers told him they came from the south and their people were called the Massylii of Numidia. Their people were nomadic horsemen. Though they could speak Greek, which most literate nations did, except for Rome, where Latin was the official language, most people spoke several languages because communication between nations was oral rather than written. So those countries that were once under the domain of Alexander the Great, Greek was most often spoken, followed by Aramaic, the language of Syria, and Mesopotamia, and Syriac, which was spoken in Antioch, one of the largest cities in the region.

Even though the brothers spoke to Titus in Greek, they told him they had their own language, which they had no name for, but historians would one day call Afro-Asiatic.

Growing up, Titus had seen a few dark-skinned people, such as the brothers, but had never known any. In ancient times there was no concept of different races, only nations and people groups. They did not seem any different, he thought, but even though they were the same age as he was, they were taller and agile. Like him, they had never fought in a war but were anxious to test their fighting skills and horsemanship. They were always smiling, joking, and boasting, as only young men who have not yet been tested in combat do, about how brave they would be the day they charged across a foreign battlefield. Titus liked them instantly.

The boys told him proudly their horses were among the oldest of breeds, called Arabians. They grew up in the desert and were highly prized, so much so that they were often brought into the family's tents for shelter and to keep them from being stolen.

Micipsa explained the Arabians were bred for their good-nature, intelligence, and willingness to please. The spirited Arabians showed alertness and fearlessness needed for skirmishes and large battles. All these traits required their owners to be skilled and respectful of their horses.

Titus asked if he could ride one of the Arabians. The brothers laughed and exchanged conspiratorial glances.

"Only we can ride them," said Gaia. "My stallion Bucephalus, named for the legendary horse of Alexander the Great, will permit no other than myself in the saddle."

"I can ride him," Titus said without bragging. "I don't know this Alexander, but I can ride your Bucephalus."

The brothers grinned and Gaia shrugged.

"Why not," he said and motioned to his horse. "There is Bucephalus. Mount him if you dare."

Titus smiled. "Dare?"

"If you are not fearful," Micipsa said.

"He is an animal. I do not fear animals. He is not my Surus, but he will do," Titus said as he approached the shimmering roan Arabian.

Micipsa and Gaia crossed their arms in anticipation of a short, humiliating ride. Titus stood before Bucephalus as the horse looked down at him curiously. Bucephalus pulled his head back when Titus reached up to touch his nose. He hummed a soothing tune as he let the horse smell his hand. The horse snorted, exhaling through its nostrils in a sign of curiosity at the boy's touch and calming tones. This human was different, interesting to the horse and he began to display a behavior of eagerness.

The brothers recognized the signs the Arabian was displaying and watched in awe as Titus effortlessly swung up on to its back. The horse was eager to run, and Titus let him have his way as they sped around the field and returned to the brothers. Titus leapt off just as the horse slid to a stop. The brothers were stunned.

"He has never permitted another on his back," Gaia exclaimed. "How were you able to do this?"

Titus shrugged playfully. "Once you ride an elephant, a horse is of little challenge."

Chapter Nine

Surus charged at the row of straw dummies dressed to resemble Roman legionnaires. Astride her neck, Titus raised his bow, let go of the string, and was drawing another arrow from the quiver as the first flew straight and true to one of the dummy's chests, right where a legionnaire's heart would have been. This was a game to Titus, and he had little understanding that he was training to kill.

"Excellent," a voice shouted from behind.

Titus turned to see Hannibal, the great general of Carthage, riding his magnificent North African Berber horse named Balius. Hannibal smiled as he rode up next to Surus.

"Please, dismount, Titus Aurelius, son of Lucius, so that I may not strain my neck looking up as we speak," Hannibal called up to the boy.

Titus touched Surus' right ear and clicked his tongue. The elephant lifted her right leg as Titus swung off her neck to the leg and then the ground. Hannibal dismounted and the boy walked boldly up to him. Hannibal was a giant of a man, powerfully built, with a bushy black beard. His skin was burned even more brown than its natural color from the sun. His brown eyes were highlighted with specs of yellow. When he removed his bronze helmet, he revealed a mass of curly black hair. He held the helmet under his right arm out of habit to keep his sword hand free. His leather and bronze armor consisted of cuirass—with the insignia of Carthage in the center—to protect his chest and greaves to protect his legs. He stood a foot taller than Titus.

"I have been watching the two of you," said Hannibal. "You and Surus are doing very well in training. And from what I just saw you will contribute greatly as a bowman." He noticed the sling and bag of stones fastened to Titus' belt. "You are a slinger, as well?"

"Yes, general," Titus answered self-consciously, his left hand touching the sling wrapped around his body for easy access.

"And the brothers, Gaia and Micipsa, inform me that you also have a way with horses." As he said this Hannibal stroked his horse Balius' nose.

"They are not elephants," Titus answered with no ill intent.

Hannibal grinned. "No, they are not elephants, but they have their uses, as do elephants." Hannibal had been watching Titus and Surus from afar from the first day at the training camp. He had seen how they had a special bond, how they communicated with each other through gestures and sounds, how they worked together as a force to be used in battle. He knew the boy had special abilities with animals, but he was too gentle to fight. The boy was small but capable of fighting as long as he was with his elephant, Hannibal thought. He was not sure how long Titus would survive in battle if he were to find himself apart from Surus. He was immediately fond of the boy and while he wished him to come to no harm, he knew many of his army were no older than Titus. Barely teenagers, they were training to be warriors. He knew many would die.

Hannibal could not help himself, though. He felt a special kinship toward Titus, perhaps because the boy reminded him of his own son Antiochus, who he dearly missed because his wife, Princess Imilce, of the Ilergetes tribe, had taken him with her to visit her family along the Hispania coast.

Together, Titus and Surus had become a formidable pair, earning the respect and admiration of the other mahouts and soldiers. The respect may have had as much to do with the fact that every member of the camp knew that Hannibal had taken them under his wing of protection. But, as small as he was, Titus impressed even the most experienced warrior as he quickly became an expert bowman. Without fail, he could hit any target, whether he was riding Surus or running beside her.

When not training, Hannibal would treat him like his own family, often inviting the boy to his tent, where he instructed Titus in the history of Carthage, politics, mathematics, philosophy, strategy, and tactics. Titus' mind had been set free by Surus and Hannibal expanded it every day.

Hannibal would speak proudly of his father's campaign against Rome, and of his brothers, Hasdrubal and Mago, who would be leading units of the army in the next fight that was planned for the following summer months. Hannibal knew intuitively that Titus was wise beyond his years and shared his vision for Carthage's rule of the known world.

Titus loved listening to Hannibal's stories and ideas. He felt a deep connection with the general, who was becoming a second father to him. He was also beginning to feel a new-found sense of belonging and loyalty to Carthage. He was not familiar with the concept of hate, but if he could muster up something akin to it, that is what he felt for Rome, which Hannibal drummed into him was the enemy of his people. He wanted to fight for Hannibal and help him achieve his goals. He wanted to make him proud and honor his name.

Titus looked at Hannibal, who was still smiling at him. He smiled back and saluted him.

"General, I, I mean we," he said as he glanced at Surus, "will fight for you, and for Carthage."

Hannibal nodded and clapped him on the shoulder.

"I know, Titus. I know. And I am glad to have you by my side," Hannibal said with genuine pride. "You and Surus are my best warriors."

Chapter Ten

During the time of their training, Titus had only been exposed to the other mahouts and their elephants and a few of the Numidian cavalry, including the two royals, Gaia and Micipsa. He had no concept of how large Hannibal's army was. As the time to launch the campaign against Rome drew closer, the elephants and handlers were exposed to other units.

He rode Surus into the camps of more than ninety thousand well-disciplined heavy infantry, who fought with spears and shields and wore helmets and breastplates for protection. As Carthaginian citizens with a personal stake in defeating Rome, they were the backbone of Hannibal's army. There were also twenty thousand light infantry from Libya, a subject to Carthage, who would fight with javelins, slings, and knives, and wore tunics and leather caps. The Numidians, he was to learn more about, would ride without saddles or bridles on their swift, agile Arabians, using spears, swords, and shields. They would be used in frontal calvary attacks, hit-and-run skirmishes, and scouting missions. There were also a few members of the Hispania and Celtic medium infantries who met with Hannibal and his brothers in preparation to joining the army with another twenty-five thousand fighters at Qart Hadasht.

Then one day Titus came upon a small camp located outside of the main camp where he met and immediately fell into accord with young warriors a little older than him called Skirmishers. These fighters were comprised of two groups: Balearic slingers and Velites. He felt a particular kinship to these boys because their main weapon of choice was the sling. He immediately fell in step with the slingers as they practiced hurling small stones with deadly accuracy over long distances, far exceeding what the average spear could be thrown. The Velites were even more impressive to him because they were beyond reckless, utterly fearless, and had no concept of death. They fought as light skirmishers, providing screens for the main infantry lines, and were particularly adept at hit-and-run tactics.

Then there were the mercenaries. These men came from many countries and fought for whomever paid them the most. While their loyalty could be bought, once they were on the payroll they would fight to the death—most of the time.

Late one evening, he sat exhausted by a campfire near the elephant pen where Surus rested peacefully. He had just finished feeding Surus, when he heard a loud and mocking voice behind him, coming from the dark.

"Hey, look who it is! It is the simple-minded lad and his ugly beast!" a voice called.

Titus turned and saw five men approaching him. They were mercenaries, hired by Hannibal's brother, General Mago. They wore mismatched armor and weapons and had scars and tattoos all over their bodies. They looked mean and dirty, and even from a distance, Titus could smell them.

Titus recognized the leader of the group. His name was Brutus, and he was a former Roman soldier who had deserted and thrown in his lot with the Carthaginians—for a price. He was tall and muscular, with a shaved head and a long beard. He had a sword in one hand and a whip in the other. He was the one who had spoken.

"What do you want, Brutus?" Titus asked, trying to sound brave, as he stood to face the men. He stroked the sling with his left hand as his right slipped a stone from the pouch on his belt.

Brutus grinned and cracked his whip. "We want to have some fun with you and your beast. You think you are something special because Hannibal has taken a liking to you."

"I'm not special," Titus said.

"You think you're better than us, just because of that elephant," Brutus mocked. "You are not. You are weak and will only get others killed because of your weakness. Without that elephant, you are nothing."

Brutus and his men laughed and jeered. Titus felt a surge of anger and fear. He loved Surus more than anything, and he hated anyone who insulted her. He also hated Brutus and his men, who were always bullying and harassing him. He wished he could stand up to them, but he knew he was no match for them. He was only a boy, and they were brutal warriors.

He looked around, hoping to see someone who could help him.

He spotted Gaia and Micipsa approaching. They had heard the commotion and were running towards him. Being the sons of King Masinissa meant nothing to the mercenaries. It would be a high mark, they thought to themselves, to beat not only this elephant boy but a couple of spoiled royals.

"What's going on?" Gaia said, knowing very well what Brutus and his men were up to. Titus grinned. Stealthily, he took a stone from the pouch and slipped it in his sling.

Brutus and his men sneered and laughed. "Oh, look who's here! It is the king's brats! What are you going to do, huh? Throw your toys at us?"

Both boys had spears and shields in their hands. Gaia looked the mercenaries over as he thought the best way to handle the situation. He glanced at his brother then stuck the spear in the ground and set the shield down. "We won't need these."

"No" Micipsa said with a shrug, as he also stuck his spear in the ground and set his shield down.

"No, we will not. Not with this bunch of overweight, drunkards, who show how brave they are by attacking our best friend," Gaia said.

Both boys had slings similar to the one Titus now had hidden behind their backs.

The mercenaries moved closer, forming a circle around them. They raised their weapons, ready to attack. The boys backed up, forming a triangle. They stood motionless but ready. Nearby, Surus and the other elephants sensed the danger and moved closer, curious.

The fight was about to begin, when a loud and authoritative voice stopped them. "What is going on here?"

Everyone turned and saw Hasdrubal striding out of the darkness toward them. He had heard the noise and had come to investigate. He looked angry and disappointed. He was a tall and handsome man, with long hair and a beard. He had a scar where his left eye had been before losing it in a firefight against Hispania rebels. He had a helmet under his arm and a gold and red cloak hung majestically from his shoulders, a sword hung at his side and a shield on his back. He was the subordinate commander of the infantry and the hero of the army. Everyone respected and feared him. But not the mercenaries, though they would have been wise to do so. But they were neither wise nor cautious.

Brutus and his men bowed their heads and lowered their weapons. They knew they were in trouble. Hasdrubal glared at them and spoke, "Brutus, explain yourself. Why are you and your men harassing these boys?"

Brutus tried to sound innocent and respectful.

"Commander, we were just having some friendly sport with them. Nothing serious. Just a bit of harmless fun. Besides, they cannot be boys if they are to fight against Rome, can they, commander?"

Hasdrubal looked from the mercenaries to the boys. *Brutus had a point*, he thought. *If they could not stand up to a bit of fun, even if it might be painful, then how would they survive in battle?* He had spotted the slings hidden behind the boys' backs and knew what was in store for the mercenaries. He winked at the three and as he turned on his heels his cape bellowed out behind him. He called back over his shoulder, "You may continue."

Brutus grinned broadly and glared hatefully at Hasdrubal's back as he disappeared into the dark beyond the light from the campfire. Then he turned back to the boys. "You may not die tonight, but you will wish you did," he said menacingly.

The five each took one step toward the boys when the three suddenly swung their slings over their heads and let the stones fly. Three of the mercenaries dropped limply in their tracks, leaving only Brutus and one other man. Surprised, the two hesitated just long enough for the boys to refill their slings. Brutus looked down at his comrades. He was not sure if they were dead or not, but he did not want to hang around long enough to join them. As he and the other man turned to run, three round stones streaked through the air and connected with the backs of their heads. They dropped limply before taking another step.

The boys looked at each other, amazed at their accomplishment and having survived without a beating. Then they turned at the sound of laughter coming from the dark and they knew General Hasdrubal had witnessed the whole incident. They grinned at one another.

Titus turned to his two friends. "I'm hungry," he said simply, as if nothing had happened.

"Nothing like a good fight to make a man's belly grumble," Micipsa joked.

"I know where the cook hides the leftovers," Maia added.

Chapter Eleven

The day finally came when the army prepared to march toward the port city of Aga El Kram, where there were two co-joined port facilities: a circular one with storehouses and loading capabilities for war ships and a second for trading vessels.

Titus felt a mix of excitement and nervousness as he watched the sun rise over the horizon. He knew that today was the day he had been waiting for. Today was his birthday. He was now fourteen. Today was also the day he and over one hundred twenty thousand others would make their way to the ships that would carry them across the sea to New Carthage, on the southern coast of Hispania as they would follow Hannibal, the hero of his people, to war against Rome.

He looked at Surus. She was calmly helping herself to a fresh load of hay. He stroked her trunk and spoke to her softly, "Today we go on an adventure."

Surus made a low rumble in her throat. She may not have understood the intent of his words, but she trusted Titus and would follow him anywhere.

Trumpets sounded in the distance and company commanders

shouted orders to form up for the march to the city. There were so many that it would take days for all of them to get there. Normally Titus liked to walk beside Surus but this morning he wanted to see the world from the height of her tall back. He picked up his spear and shield, then tapped her trunk. She curled it so he could step on it, then she hoisted him up to her back.

He was a soldier now in Hannibal's army, and he was proud of it. He looked around and saw his friends, Gaia and Micipsa, who were riding their magnificent Arabians among the rest of the cavalry. They waved and grinned as they joined their unit. The army had been training and preparing for months, gathering equipment, food, and supplies. They had been waiting for the right moment, the right season, the right wind. And now, the moment had come.

In the port and at sea hundreds of huge ships were waiting for them. They were the finest ships in the world, built by the best craftsmen and engineers. They were fast and strong, and some of the larger ones, called quinqueremes could carry thousands of men, animals, and supplies. They were the pride of Carthage, and they were the key to Hannibal's plan.

His plan was bold and brilliant. He wanted to invade Italia, the heart of Rome, and strike at the enemy where they least expected it. The army would cross the Mediterranean Sea, the Pyrenees, the Alps, and the rivers, facing challenges and dangers along the way. They would do what no other army had ever done before, and what no one would ever do again.

It would be historic and tragic. Over the next weeks the army marched to the outskirts of Aga El Kram. When they passed through town the crowds lined the streets and cheered them on. Banners and flags waved from every window. Even the statues of gods and heroes seemed to cheer them on. Many had never seen the beauty and magnificence of Carthage, and they felt a surge of pride and love. They also felt a pang of sadness and nostalgia, as they knew many of them would not return.

They reached the port city, and they saw the ships lined up along the docks. They were amazed by the sight. There were hundreds of ships, of assorted sizes and shapes. Some were small and swift, for scouting and raiding. Some were medium and sturdy, for transporting and fighting. Some were large and majestic, commanding, and inspiring. And some were gigantic and extraordinary, for carrying the formidable army, including thirty-seven elephants.

Titus was assigned to one of the giant ships, which required a citizen crew of seven thousand to row and protect it. Hundreds of mercenary soldiers were bivouacked on lower decks. They would supplement the ship's crews with loading, unloading, and defending the ship against Roman warships. They had to work hard and fast, as they had to leave the docks to move out to sea to make way for other ships to be loaded. They would wait at anchor for the entire fleet of over nine hundred ships to begin the journey across the Mediterranean.

Titus led Surus up the gangway to the ship. The huge deck was covered with ropes and nets. They saw the large cages that were built to hold the oxen and other animals that would feed the army along the way. Surus and two other elephants were taken below decks where large stalls had been built for them. Bens of hay and barrels of water were nearby. There were also stalls for the horses. Some men would stay with the animals to feed and tend to them. Titus rigged a hammock for himself in Surus' pen. She was taking the whole journey in stride and her gentle throat rumbling seemed to soothe the other elephants.

When it was time to move the ship, the sailors went through the decks to let everyone know they should be prepared for the rough ride to come. *No matter how large the ship, the sea is always more powerful,* they warned the landlubbers who had never been to sea. Many wondered how the elephants would react when the ship started swaying and pitching. They were to soon find out.

Chapter Twelve

Two days out to sea the ships were hit by a raging storm that, if not for the Carthaginian's skilled seamanship borne of over four hundred years of sailing throughout the Mediterranean, could have sunk the entire fleet. At the first sign of gale winds the crew aboard each ship lowered the sails. The thousands of men at the oars had to stay at their stations to keep the vessels moving through the rain and giant swells and deep troughs. To help steady each ship sea anchors made of conical-shaped fabric were tossed overboard tied to long ropes from each ship's bow. These clever devices provided hydrodynamic drag that kept the ships from turning sideways and being swamped.

The fleet would have to make the round trip between Carthage and Hispania a dozen or more times to transport the entire army, camp followers, and animals and supplies.

The average Carthaginian ship was one hundred fifty feet long and seventeen feet wide. Each had hundreds of men rowing on multiple decks stacked above one another. By comparison, the ship carrying the elephants was gargantuan at over three hundred feet long by thirty-five feet wide. When at sea the crew numbered over seven thousand, comprised of the compliment of two hundred fifty sailors with the bulk of men rowing being soldiers.

On the lowermost of four decks Titus and Surus were in the large stall. Other elephants were in similar enclosures with high gates and side walls. For safety, the elephants' tusks were wrapped in layers of heavy linen, bound by ropes. Each elephant's front legs were hobbled with heavy rope. Additional ropes were fastened around the animals' bodies and secured to large metal bolts in the decks to keep them from moving. Since elephants seldom laid down, even to sleep, they would make most of the week-long journey standing in place.

Titus and the other mahouts cared for the elephants with feed, water, and soothing words. They stayed close to the elephants by sleeping in hammocks stretched between poles just outside the pens. When the ships began to violently pitch and sway from the storm the elephants were less stressed than some of the men, mainly because Titus had brewed tea made from chamomile flowers to give to the elephants to keep them blissfully sedated.

In another ship hundreds of cavalrymen and their Arabians were not so tranquil. The horses were penned in tightly together with their front legs hobbled. Naturally high strung, if not for the hobbles and being pressed together in tight quarters they would have trampled one another to death.

Some of the camp followers were in the same ship. One small group was a Syrian family comprised of the father, who was a sometime blacksmith and served in the army with his bow, his wife, and two daughters. The oldest daughter, who was fourteen, was named Cleopatra. She was not named after the co-regent of Egypt and mistress of Julius Caesar, who would not be born for another one hundred thirty-eight years, but for Cleopatra of Macedon, the sister of Alexander the Great, who was born one hundred thirty-seven years prior to the Carthaginian invasion now being launched against Rome.

Cleopatra, if she had been born a male, would surely have been a warrior. She was a warrior at heart and her father encouraged her to train as one. She grew up on stories of the Amazon Queen Penthesilea, who was said to be the daughter of Ares, the god of war, and came from the area of the Black Sea and fought against the Greeks during the Trojan War. She was murdered by Achilles, over nine hundred years ago.

In later centuries, historians would declare that Amazon women warriors, the Trojan War, and Achilles were only myths, but to Cleopatra they were her history, though she never read of such events and people but heard the tales that had been passed down through generations of storytellers.

Her father taught her the use of the bow, and her new friends, two brothers who were in the calvary, taught her to ride the Arabians while training those months in Carthage. In just the few weeks during training at the camps, she had mastered shooting with the bow and arrows while riding bareback at full gallop. Another warrior, eager for her attention, also taught her the fine techniques of swordsmanship. In her tiny, compact frame she was a fierce warrior to be reckoned with, if only given the chance by the men who controlled every aspect of her existence.

The elephants may have been tranquilized by the flowery drug, but the men and women, horses, oxen, and other livestock were miserable and terrified. Humans and animals were wet, cold, hungry, and seasick. They had no space to move or breathe, and they had to endure the constant noise and smells. The people wished they were on land, or at least on a calmer sea. They prayed to the gods for mercy and protection. Those who were not on duty or tending to animals tied themselves up as best they could in their bunks or hammocks to keep from being thrown across the rooms, which could be fatal.

When he left the dank and musky decks below and made his way up to the weather deck, Titus noticed that the only ones who were enjoying the ride were the ship's captain or trierarcho and his crew. They were all experienced sailors, who knew how to handle a ship in a storm and had fought many battles at sea against Rome and other nations. They were just too busy keeping the ship stable and afloat to worry. As citizen sailors, they were also loyal to Hannibal, and they believed in his cause. They were proud and confident, and they were ready to face any challenge or danger.

The captain was standing on the bridge as he kept watch for possible enemy ships. In this case, the enemy was any Roman vessel. He looked at the sky and the sea, and he spoke to his helmsman, who was standing next to him. "Looks like we're in for a rough night," he said rhetorically.

"We've seen worse, haven't we, sir," the helmsman replied, also rhetorically.

"I'm worried about those elephants," the captain said as he gazed through the downpour. The helmsman stared ahead into the squall, waiting for the captain to finish what he was saying.

"They're unpredictable and dangerous. They also weigh far too much to calculate the counterweight for the opposite side of the ship from where the animals are kept. No two of them weigh the same, so how are we supposed to know if the ship is balanced?"

"She seems to be riding steady enough, sir."

"I will be at ease when we get them out of the ship, and we are headed back home. No more elephants if I have anything to say about it."

Chapter Thirteen

The next morning the storm had passed, and the sea was calm. No wind filled the sails. Only the sound of a drumbeat, and the dipping of hundreds of synchronized oars indicated the ship was moving.

Cleopatra had just stepped onto the weather deck when she heard the call from high in the mast, "Sail on the horizon, captain."

She ran to the railing and looked in the direction the lookout was pointing. Just coming over the horizon was a single square sail. The rising sun cast a glow through the sail, and she saw the wolf's head silhouette. She looked at the captain.

"Is it Roman?" she asked quietly.

"It is," he said calmly, eagerly.

"Will you fight?"

"They seem intent on it."

"Can we outrun them?"

"Why would we do that?" he said.

"There are families onboard."

"They are Carthaginians," he said as if their citizenship explained everything as he studied her. "I have seen you practicing with the bow. Perhaps you should get it before those Roman pigs catch up with us."

"Where's the rest of the fleet?" she asked.

He scanned the sea, "Not here," he said as if joking.

"You think this is amusing?" she asked.

"If one is not prepared to die, then one should not go to sea." He looked toward the ship fast approaching. "Now would be a good time to arm yourself, young woman." He turned to the crewman next to him. "Quartermaster, sound all hands to station, now."

As Cleopatra went below decks to retrieve her weapons, the quartermaster took a hammer and started banging on a metal drum. Soon, crewmen and passengers rushed up on deck. All were armed.

The captain shouted orders down an open hatch to the man called the *hortatory* to beat a cadence on his drums to pick up the pace to synchronize the strokes of the hundreds of rowers. Cleopatra returned to the deck with her bow and arrows, and a sword strapped to her back, and stood alongside her father who had his weapons ready. He looked down at her with a mixture of pride and fatalism.

"I pray to the gods to protect us and for victory," he said. "If they do not, then may we take many Romans to hades with us."

The Roman ship noticeably increased its speed as it drew nearer. It was small and fast, a scout ship sent out to harass and disrupt shipping from competing nations. The captain and the quartermaster exchanged a look, and they smiled. They had been waiting for this moment. They had been itching for a fight. They were ready to face the enemy. The captain knew he had a good and brave crew, and when he looked at the caliber of the men and women who came up on deck from below, he saw all were armed and there was no panic on their faces. *This would be a good day to fight or die*, he thought.

The crew and passengers began to shout and beat on shields or clang swords and knives together in anticipation as the hundreds of oars on both sides of the ship dipped into the sea, propelling the long ship directly at the Romans. The captain grabbed his sword and shield, as did the quartermaster. Cleopatra and her father notched arrows and watched as the Roman ship aimed its bow at the starboard oars.

"Bring her about to ram," the captain called calmly.

"Aye, sir," said the quartermaster as he guided the ship, which was twice the length of the Roman ship, giving the Carthaginians the advantage as the bow slammed through the oars on the port side of the Roman ship. When the oars exploded from the impact screams of the Roman rowers could be heard. A moment later, the Roman ship's bow crushed the oars on the Carthaginian ship's starboard side.

Flaming arrows arched across from the Roman ship setting small fires wherever they struck the Carthaginian ship.

"Fire, now," ordered the captain.

Cleopatra released her arrow. She watched it fly its deadly path onto the Roman ship where it struck a young sailor in the neck. For just a moment she regretted taking the shot, but as more Roman arrows began to land, some of the people fell under their deadly impacts, she pulled another arrow from the quiver and sent it flying at a Roman crewman high up in the mast who was shooting arrows down at her people. Her arrow flew true and struck the man in the chest. He screamed as he fell into the sea.

The broken oars of both ships locked them in a deadly embrace. Then the Romans lowered their secret weapon called the *corvus*, a wooden ramp with metal spikes that hooked onto the Carthaginian ship as Roman soldiers poured aboard.

The Carthaginian crew cheered and rushed at the Romans with axes, spears, and javelins. Their bloodlust equaled that of the Romans. They loved a good fight as much as they hated the Romans.

Cleopatra fired her arrows as the Romans rushed across the deck, cutting down crewmen and civilians. The captain and quartermaster stood their ground and struck down several Romans before they were also cut down. A half dozen Romans fell to her arrows before she ran out. Without hesitation, she dropped the bow and pulled her sword from its sheath. She saw her father fall from a Roman ax and killed the man who swung it. She had the advantage of reach with her long sword over the Romans' gladius or short swords and drew blood over and over.

Just as it looked like the Carthaginians were about to overpower the surviving Romans a terrible crashing sound brought the fight to a sudden stop. As the Carthaginians turned to see what was happening behind them a second Roman ship tore through the side of the ship, splintering the hull and crushing hundreds below decks. The Roman ship with a bronze ram called a *rostrum* attached to the bow continued

through the Carthaginian ship, splitting it in half. Romans and Carthaginians were flung through the air or mangled in the wreckage.

The last thing Cleopatra remembered as she was thrown over the side and into the sea was what would happen to her mother and little sister.

Chapter Fourteen

Cleopatra was alone and afraid.

The Carthaginian ship and the thousands aboard, as well as the two Roman ships and their crews, had perished. She did not know how long she had been in the water as she clung to a small piece of wood as if it were life itself. She was exhausted as the hot sun beat down on her. The sea to her culture was full of monsters and evil. She was more afraid of what might rise from the depths than drowning. Her strength was leaving her body and before she knew what was happening, she lost her hold on the wooden timber that had been keeping her afloat. Panic was beginning to take a grip on her when she heard something behind her.

She was a strong swimmer but even the strongest swimmer would eventually surrender and slip below the surface. The sound of some creature behind her was too much to ignore. She forced herself to turn in the water to face whatever demon had come from below to devour her. Instead, she was stunned to see a white horse swimming effortlessly toward her. It snorted a friendly greeting as it came up beside her and stayed there until she reached out and clutched two handfuls of its long mane and pulled herself on its back.

“Where did you come from,” she gasped.

The white horse snorted in response and started swimming.

She had fallen asleep and when she woke, she was still clutching the horse’s mane as it swam strongly toward a setting sun. *How many hours had she been swimming*, Cleopatra wondered in awe at the horse’s stamina. It did not seem to be tired in the least and it also seemed to know where it was going.

A lookout high in the mast called out as he pointed east. Men ran to the railing to see what he had spotted. *Was it a Roman ship?* Titus joined the curious onlookers. As the ship slowed to a stop they looked down at the body of a girl. She appeared to be lifeless. No man ventured to jump into the sea to retrieve her body. They may sail the sea, but none would voluntarily leap into it. Not being a sailor but having often ventured into the rapids of the rivers of Carthage, Titus had no knowledge or fear of the sea’s monsters.

He climbed over the rail and leapt into the water near the body. As he reached under her arms to hold her close to him as he swam back to the ship, he was startled when she took a deep breath and opened her brown eyes to gaze into his. She said nothing but would not take her eyes off his face.

The sailors lowered a rope ladder to the water and two men ventured down to help bring the girl up on deck. They laid her down on her back. Titus knelt beside her.

“You are safe,” he said.

"What of the horse?" she asked in a soft voice. "Did you save her too?"

"We saw no horse," he said. "You were alone."

"No," she said as she struggled to rise. Titus helped her to her feet and over to the railing. She looked across the water, confused. "There was a horse. She saved me."

"Maybe you imagined—"

"No, there was a horse, and she stayed with me and carried me all day."

"Perhaps it was Poseidon's hippocamp," Titus said.

"A seahorse?" came the voice of Hasdrubal.

Titus turned to look at the man who had recruited him and Surus, who he admired and loved, almost as much as he honored Hannibal.

"That would explain how she survived so long in the sea. Only a seahorse could swim so long and then disappear without a trace," Titus said.

Cleopatra looked skeptically at Titus. "It was a Thessalian mare and no seahorse," she said.

"Are you so sure," Hasdrubal asked. "No one else saw this white horse you claim saved you. Perhaps it was only your imagination."

"I did not imagine this," she said and held up a handful of white hair. She gave her life for me."

Suddenly, the voice of the lookout called out, "Wreckage off the port beam."

Hasdrubal and Titus, and several crewmen went to the rail and spied a man floating on wreckage. Two sailors climbed down the side of the ship to retrieve the man and when he set foot on the deck Hasdrubal was surprised that he knew the man.

"General, it is not every day that such a noble Roman as yourself finds himself aboard a ship of Hannibal," Hasdrubal said as the battered soldier stood before him on wobbly legs. "You seem to have lost your ship, and your command."

The general glared at Hasdrubal and eyed the men standing behind him. Then he spotted the lone woman among them. "You," he said in amazement. "You are alive?"

Hasdrubal and Titus turned to see Cleopatra glaring at the man. "You know this woman?" Hasdrubal asked.

"Know her," the general said in shock. "She killed many of my men with her bow and more with her sword. She is no mortal to slay so many and yet survive."

"Cleopatra, come forward," Hasdrubal said.

Cleopatra stepped forward hesitantly until she stood between Hasdrubal and Titus. "Is what the general said true, you slew his men with bow and sword?" he asked.

Cleopatra stared defiantly at the Roman. "Apparently one too few since he is standing before you," she said boldly.

Hasdrubal's mouth opened in amazement, but no words came out. Titus smiled at her. She smiled back at him, and it was plain to

Hasdrubal that the two young people had already connected in their hearts. He turned back to the general.

"You may as well know the name of the warrior who drew Roman blood this day. She is Cleopatra of Syria." Then he turned to Cleopatra. "And may I introduce to you General Publius Cornelius Scipio." He smiled at Cleopatra. "You have done well this day, Cleopatra, Amazon queen of Syria. You have not only drawn first blood in this little war, but you have brought to heel the highest-ranking council of the Roman Republic." He turned back to Scipio. "One has to wonder why such an important Roman citizen was aboard a navy longa (long ship in Latin)."

Scipio remained tight-lipped as he glared at Cleopatra with hatred.

"Not important, I suppose, since you are without a ship and are now my *guest*," Hasdrubal said, as he looked at Cleopatra and Titus. "No harm will come to you as long as you are on this ship. Tomorrow we will rejoin the fleet, and my good brother will have words with you. Come, join me below for food and wine."

Scipio bowed slightly. "I would be honored, Commander."

As Hasdrubal led the senator-general below decks to his cabin the whispers were already beginning about the amazing female warrior who slew tens, perhaps hundreds of Roman soldiers. In a week's time, as word spread through the fleet and to Hannibal, Cleopatra was being hailed as the new Amazon queen, so named by Hasdrubal himself, who had *drawn first blood against the hated Romans, and would fight with Carthage and kill many more Romans*, they said.

Titus admired Cleopatra but did not see her as a queen or Amazon. He knew there was something different about her, as there was about himself. He was attracted to her in a way he did not understand. What he did understand, however, was that Cleopatra seemed to want to stay with him and when she informed Hannibal of this he declared that the Amazon queen was under his protection and no man should dare approach her with anything but honorable intensions. He also declared that Titus would be her guardian and companion from that day forward. As for her intensions, Cleopatra knew in her heart that one day Titus and she would wed. But for now, they had an adventure to experience, a war to fight, and Romans to vanquish.

But first, Titus thought, he must introduce Cleopatra to Surus. If Surus approved of this woman then Titus was prepared to have her at his side, wherever they might be.

Chapter Fifteen

The full moon hung over the coast of Hispania. It silhouetted Hannibal's fleet of nine hundred ninety-nine ships as they sailed in calm waters along the coast to the city of Ampurias, founded in 575 BC by Phocaea colonists. Hannibal had a loyal ally there, King Indibilis of the Ilergetes tribe, an ancient Iberian people who lived in the region of Ausona, near the Ebro River.

Hasdrubal, with his brother Mago and nephew Hanno, oversaw the offloading of the army, which took more than two weeks. There were no docks, so the soldiers, camp followers, livestock, and elephants were carefully offloaded onto barges to transport them to the shore. While Hannibal led the four-hundred-mile march south over the next two months to New Carthage, the two brothers and their nephew spread out along the miles-long convoy to carry out Hannibal's orders. Along the way, they captured several Roman occupied cities.

Hannibal instructed them to find a suitable location outside of New Carthage, where they could set up a large and secure base camp. The camp was massive to accommodate the thousands of men, material, and camp followers, along with thousands of animals that included livestock, horses, and the seventeen African elephants that were added to the twenty Indian elephants already in New Carthage. He also told them to prepare for the march ahead, which would be long and perilous. All four were veterans of Hamilcar's war (First Punic War) against Rome and knew they faced many dangers along the way, not only from the natural obstacles of the mountains, but also from the hostile tribes that would try to attack and harass them.

Meanwhile, in the camp, Titus was looking for his friends, Gaia and Micipsa. They were the only ones he had become friendly with over the months of training for war in Carthage, and he wanted to introduce them to Cleopatra. Since her family had been killed by the Romans, and he had rescued her from the sea, she remained close to him at all times. *It was not quite love yet*, she thought, *but it was close*. Titus was not sure what to call the feelings he was beginning to have for her. He felt strange when around her. The only women he had known were his mother and sisters. Then there was Surus, *but she did not count*, he thought.

He discovered the Numidian cavalry was in a different camp several miles away. Since they did not have horses and they did not feel overly safe walking in unfamiliar country, Titus suggested they make the journey aboard Surus.

Aboard the ship, when he told her he wanted to introduce her to Surus, at first Cleopatra thought it strange that she needed to be formerly introduced to an animal. But once she met Surus she understood. She knew that Surus was no ordinary elephant, not that Cleopatra, never having been around elephants before, understood one elephant from another. But it was obvious to her that Surus was not only massive in size she had a massive heart when it came to Titus. Her love was obvious, Cleopatra understood their bond after witnessing the show of affection the elephant demonstrated toward Titus through her throaty rumbles, gentle caresses with her trunk, and wanting to be as physically close to the young man as she could be.

They were quite the sight as the two of them rode Surus through the countryside and the outskirts of the town. The people were becoming used to seeing elephants but none the size and speed of Surus.

When they entered the cavalry encampment Titus recognized the flag of the Numidian king and knew the boys would be there if not riding their beloved Arabians.

Riding an eighteen-thousand-pound elephant through camp caused quite a commotion alerting the brothers to step out of the tent. Through mouthfuls of meat, they grinned at the sight of Titus and Surus and hailed him with colorful curses. Then they noticed Cleopatra sitting behind Titus. They turned around to spit out the meat and wiped their mouths and chins on their sleeves before turning back to ogle the beautiful Syrian girl.

In a camp with few women other than the wives or slaves of some of the older, more senior men, Cleopatra's beauty almost hurt their eyes for straining them to see all of her. The boys ran up beside Surus to give her a hand as she was climbing down the elephant's trunk. The boys tried to jostle each other aside to offer her a hand down.

She looked at them as if they were acting crazy, which they were because no young man would go out his way—except for his mother or a sister— to help a woman in this society.

"What are you two up to?" Titus quizzed the brothers as he stepped off Surus' trunk.

"Who might this beauty be," Gaia asked eagerly.

"I saw her first," chimed in Micipsa.

Cleopatra smiled coquettishly if that were in a Syrian warrior woman's feminine arsenal. But she was not one to flirt with strange men, much less boys.

"Cleopatra," Titus said in introduction.

"Cleopatra of Macedonia?" Micipsa asked as his brother nudged him in the ribs.

"It is a common enough name where I come from," she said.

"Where might that be," Gaia asked.

"Syria," she answered.

"I have always heard Syrian women are exceptionally beautiful," Gaia said, grinning, adding with a leer, "and agile."

"Are you the Amazon so many are speaking of in the camps?" Micipsa asked in awe. "The one who drew first Roman blood."

Titus stepped up next to Cleopatra. "The same," he said with pride as she gave him a warm smile.

The brothers noticed their exchange of glances. They looked at one another with a role of the eyes, relinquishing any thought of capturing her heart, which had already been given to Titus, though, which they imagined he was not even aware of. He was too good a friend for them to think of poaching the one female in camp worth pursuing.

"You are our good friend Titus' woman, then," Micipsa asked.

"No," Titus said a little too hurriedly, as Cleopatra said simultaneously, "Yes." They exchanged a look.

"You are only a girl," Titus said unconvincingly.

"Are you not a man?" she said haughtily.

"Of course," Titus said.

"Are you not fourteen?" she continued.

"Yes," he answered, not sure where she was headed.

"I am also fourteen," she said. "Therefore, I am a woman, not a girl who needs your protection."

"I did not mean—"

"Are we not together, by General Hannibal's decree?"

"I suppose."

"You're in it now, my friend," Gaia joked.

"In what?"

"I may not be your woman, but we are together," Cleopatra continued. "Officially."

Titus shook his head, unsure of what he was agreeing to. "I suppose."

"We are one, the two of us," she declared triumphantly. "We rode a long way, and I am hungry."

The brothers exchanged a curious look and glanced at Titus, and then Gaia motioned toward their camp. "Come, we have fresh pig on a spit."

As they sat near the fire for warmth, watching their meal roast, Cleopatra eyed it and said, "It is—small."

The brothers acted embarrassed at the size of the pig. "It is all the farmer was willing to sell us," Micipsa said.

"You could not hunt something, a little bigger," Titus said, stifling a laugh.

"After two months camped here the army has killed every hoofed animal or winged creature in the forests and meadows," Gaia said. "General Barca, that is, Hannibal, will not permit the taking of provisions from the city or farms without payment. We will soon run out of gold and food if the army stays here. There are too many of us to provide for."

"Then I have good news," said Titus. "Before coming to see you, the other General Barca, the brother, Hasdrubal, told our camp that we would be leaving for Italia in two days time. Time to pack up."

The brothers grinned. Micipsa cut off a piece of meat and handed it to Cleopatra. She nodded to him. Titus was not sure he liked her recognizing Micipsa. But *she was not his woman, no matter what she said*, he thought, though he was not sure if he believed that.

Chapter Sixteen

The next night, Titus and the brothers decided to meet up at the edge of the town. For whatever reason, Cleopatra decided to stay behind. It did not matter to the boys. She would just get in the way, they reasoned. They wanted to have some fun and create some mischief before the army moved on. They planned to sneak into the town to see if they could find some food, wine, or entertainment. They also wanted to spy on the locals and see if they could learn anything useful or interesting.

They were about to enter town when they saw a group of men approaching them. They stepped into the shadows and watched the men. They could not understand what they were saying. Not speaking the Celtic language but recognizing it, they knew the men were Gauls, who were enemies or friends of Carthaginians and Romans, alike, depending on their mood and who was paying them the most. The boys wondered what the Gauls were doing there and decided to follow them.

The Gauls were spies, sent by Consul Scipio, who Hannibal foolishly released shortly after he stepped ashore. Hasdrubal argued they should kill Scipio, but Hannibal vetoed the idea in favor of, hopefully, securing a potential ally in the Roman army. Such would not be the case and, ultimately, Scipio would eventually be Hannibal's downfall.

Today, though, the Gauls had observed Hannibal's movements and reported back to Scipio who was aboard a small ship hiding in a cove a few miles from the town. They had disguised themselves as merchants and had managed to enter the town undetected. They had also bribed some of the locals, who had agreed to help them in exchange for money and promises. They had learned that Hannibal's army would be leaving the next day. It was the easiest money they would earn, for it was not a secret at all because an army of over one hundred twenty thousand does not just disappear one morning.

It would take days for the entire army to depart, and months to reach the Pyrenees. It would be no easy march they reasoned because they had made the crossing many times themselves. And even if the army managed the Pyrenees, the Gauls knew it would be a challenging task to cross the Rhone River, especially with elephants. And then the Alps were a whole different matter. This time of year, they knew the most likely route the army would take was the Col de la Traversette pass, meaning transversus in Latin, because it was often used by the Romans coming into Hispania.

They tried to blend in with the crowds. They walked towards the camp, observing, and listening to everything they could. They saw Hannibal and his brothers riding through the camp, inspecting the troops, and giving orders. They heard Hannibal's speeches, in which he praised his soldiers for their courage and loyalty and urged them to follow him to glory and victory. They also heard some rumors and complaints from some of the soldiers who were unhappy with the harsh conditions and the uncertain outcome of the expedition.

The Gauls gathered as much information as they could and hoped to find someone to get a message to Scipio, warning him of Hannibal's intentions and movements. They knew that Hannibal was a formidable enemy, and that Rome had to be ready for the coming war. When he arrived at New Carthage, he was welcomed by the friendly inhabitants, who offered him supplies and reinforcements.

Now, Hannibal was ready to embark on the most ambitious and dangerous journey of his life, knowing that he would be lucky if half of those men entrusting in his leadership survived it would be a miracle.

Greek historian Polybius, who wrote *The Histories*, a collection of forty books between 167 BC and 146 BC, on the universal history of the Roman and the Mediterranean world, witnessed some of the following events thirty-four years before when he was just eighteen. He did not cross the Alps with Hannibal but later wrote about the campaign after he walked the entire one-thousand mile-route, from Turin, Italia, where Hannibal most likely exited the Alps, back to New Carthage, in the province of Hispania Citerior, where the march began.

In his third book of the surviving five, he wrote: "*When the appointed day arrived, Hannibal got his army in motion, which consisted of ninety-thousand infantry and about twelve-thousand cavalry. After crossing the Iber, he set about subduing the tribes of the*

Ilurgetes and Bargusii, as well as the Aerenosii and Andosini, as far as the Pyrenees. When he had reduced all this country under his power, and taken certain towns by storm, which he did with unexpected rapidity, though not without severe fighting and serious loss; he left Hanno in chief command of all the district north of the Iber, and with absolute authority over the Burgusii, who were the people that gave him most uneasiness on account of their friendly feeling towards Rome. He then detached from his army ten thousand foot and a thousand horse for the service of Hanno, —to whom also he entrusted the heavy baggage of the troops that were to accompany himself, —and the same number to go to their own land. The object of this last measure was twofold: he thereby left a certain number of well-affected persons behind him; and also held out to the others a hope of returning home, both to those Iberians who were to accompany him on his march, and to those also who for the present were to remain at home, so that there might be a general alacrity to join him if he were ever in want of a reinforcement. He then set his remaining troops in motion unencumbered by heavy baggage, fifty-thousand infantry, and nine-thousand cavalry, and led them through the Pyrenees to the passage of the river Rhone. The army was not so much numerous, as highly efficient, and in an extraordinary state of physical training from their continuous battles with the Iberians.

Hannibal left his encampments in the early summer of 219 BC and marched north, following the Ebro River. As the opening salvo of the war, he besieged the Roman-allied city of Saguntum near the coast. This triggered the Second Punic War. Eight months later, the city fell, and he massacred most of the inhabitants and plundered its wealth. He was wounded in the thigh but recovered quickly. Its coffers filled with gold and other loot, by the fall of 218 BC the army was on the move toward the Pyrenees.

As the head of the column approached the foot of the Pyrenees the rear of the column, which included the supply wagons and camp followers, was still many miles behind. It was guarded by the contingent of cavalry interspersed with four-hundred mercenary infantry soldiers. Just as the day was ending and the rear guard was building fires and setting up camp for the night, guttural screaming came out of the dark and the camp was under attack.

Women and children screamed and dashed for cover under the wagons as Allobroges marauders, a Gallic tribe loyal to Rome that lived nearby and made their living robbing and killing unfortunate souls as they were just beginning the six-thousand-five-hundred-foot ascent over the Pyrenees, attacked.

Gaia and Micipsa, along with hand-picked men, had been assigned by Hanno as the rear guard and they were ready for the attack as they grabbed bows and arrows and launched themselves onto the bare backs of their Arabians, steering them with knees and no halters or bridles.

The Allobroges were fearless and always hungry because they grew little food of their own and only ate what they could steal, so the food in the wagons was highly prized, and more than worth dying for. There were more than six hundred of them and they ignored those who fell from the shower of arrows that rained down on them as the Numidian cavalry rode into their midst firing directly at the tribesmen.

It was far from a one-way confrontation, though, as the Allobroges were experienced fighters with swords, spears, javelins, slings, and bows. They brought down many of the cavalry and more than a few of their horses as they rode past. The battle was a jumbled mass of bloodied bodies and mayhem, and it was beginning to look like the Allobroges were getting the upper hand when everyone's attention was torn from the fight as the Carthaginian infantry charged, overwhelming those Allobroges still capable of fighting.

Gaia had been wounded by an arrow through the arm, and Micipsa was struck by a rock in the side of his face thrown from a sling but still up for the fight. This was their first taste of war, and they had no fear of death. They were caught up in the bloodletting and were in no mood to take prisoners. Out of arrows, they pulled their swords and charged at any Allobroges warrior they could reach.

Hanno rode up as the last of the Allobroges was being put to the sword. Micipsa rode up to him a saluted, "General," he greeted his superior officer.

"What have you to report," Hanno said as he eyed the carnage scattered over the field.

"The enemy has been destroyed. There are thirty-three Numidian cavalry and fifty-two infantry dead, sir."

"So many?"

"There were more than six hundred who attacked. They wanted the supplies enough to die for."

"I am pleased that you assisted them in doing so," Hanno said.

Micipsa smiled. “Our pleasure, general.” He nodded toward the wagons. “The supplies and our people are safe.”

“Good. What is your name soldier?”

“Micipsa, brother of Gaia, who also fought this day, and son of King Masinissa of Numidia,” he answered with pride.

“When you next see your father, tell him I said you fought well this day. I will inform my brother of yours and your brother’s victory over of the Allobroges this day.”

“Thank you, general. It was nothing.”

“Only one as young as yourself would say thus after—” He glanced again at all the bodies strewn over the field, “such an accomplishment. Take care and keep vigil.”

“Yes, general,” Micipsa said and saluted Hanno, as the general turned his horse and galloped away.

Micipsa grinned when Gaia rode up beside him. “What was that about,” Gaia asked.

“He just wanted to say what a good job we did,” Micipsa said.

“It would have been nice if he would have joined us with his personal guard,” Gaia responded. “It was a little close there for awhile. You know you are wounded, right.” He pointed at the blood seeping from Micipsa chest wound. “Perhaps Cleopatra can tend to it.” He winked.

Chapter Seventeen

It took twenty days to cross the Pyrenees. For the most part, it was uneventful. There was still plenty of food and rations in the wagons. Less than halfway across the mountains the army stopped at several meadows along the way. The army was strewn out for miles along the twisting, narrow trail.

In one lush meadow where a stream poured into a lake at one end and cascaded over a waterfall at the other, Titus made a makeshift enclosure to bed down Surus with plenty of feed readily available around the lake. Then he and Cleopatra joined a party of hunters looking to supplement their dried meats and fruits.

There were few travelers through the Pyrenees this time of the year and the wildlife was plentiful and practically tame. They discovered a brown bear, surprising it as it was emerging from its den. They were as surprised as the bear when he suddenly charged at them. Cleopatra was first to let fly an arrow that flew true, striking the growling bear in the upper chest. It spun around angrily, biting at the arrow until it broke the shaft, then renewed its charge.

Titus juggled his spear between his hands as the bear closed the distance between them. Cleopatra was notching another arrow. The bear surprised her at its speed. She was raising her bow as it leapt at her. Suddenly, Titus was kneeling in front of her with the spear tip pointed up and the end firmly planted in the ground. Cleopatra took an involuntary step backward as the bear impaled itself on the spear. Titus pushed the spear aside and grabbed his sword, but there was no need. The bear was dead.

"It will make a fine coat for when we cross the Alps," he said more calmly than he felt.

"Who do you expect to skin it and tailor this coat?" Cleopatra said, catching her breath after the near disaster.

He looked at her and smiled. "I will skin. You sew."

"And who shall wear it?"

"I already have a coat," he said.

She smiled slightly. "Good."

The other hunters brought back three more bears, dozens of chamois antelopes, and hundreds of ptarmigans that for the lack of human contact did not bother to take flight before the hunters' slings dropped them where they grazed. Women took children to fish in nearby rivers and lakes as they camped near them. The fish were as inexperienced with humans as wildlife, and the people brought back baskets full of zebra trout, salmon, carp, and chub.

That first night in the meadow, they roasted their bounty over hundreds of fires. Gaia and Micipsa sought out Titus and Cleopatra to share the festive meal. They brought a Greek boy with them they had met before the army ventured into the mountain pass.

"This is Polybius, son of Lycortas, from Megalopolis, a fine city in Arcadia. That would be Greece, for the unlearned," Gaia offered as an introduction. Titus paid no attention to the slight; Cleopatra glared at Gaia. He grinned back at her and shrugged. He did not care what she thought.

"Welcome Polybius, son of Lycortas," Titus said light-heartedly. "What brings you to this little war our great General Hannibal is hosting?"

The brothers seemed impressed at Titus' somewhat poetic description of the impending war. Cleopatra continued to glare at the two of them.

"He fancies himself a scribe," Micipsa interjected as he slapped Polybius on the back and pointed to an empty spot by the fire. Polybius sat and Cleopatra handed him a plate of food.

"Thank you," he said to her, then offered to the boys, "A chronicler."

"Chronicler?" Titus said, confused.

"Historian, I suppose," Polybius said.

"What does an army need of a historian," Micipsa quizzed him.

Polybius chewed on a drumstick and looked at his four new friends. "The army does not require my services as a historian. It only needs my good right arm to throw a spear or use a sling. If I should survive, I hope the future will be in need of the particulars of how this great adventure unfolded."

"Adventure," Titus said.

"Yes, adventure," Polybius said enthusiastically. "What your great Hannibal Barca is attempting has never been done before. He has gathered one of the largest forces in history, with the purpose of going through Rome's back door over the Alps. No one will be expecting it. He will be victories, especially," he looked over his shoulder at Surus, grazing peacefully nearby, "with your magnificent elephants. How many are there?"

"Thirty-seven," Titus said.

"They will terrify the legions," Polybius said confidently.

"That's the plan," said Micipsa.

Titus smiled, not so sure what the plan was.

A week later, when they came out of the mountains and entered a long valley rich in crops that was the entrance into a region of Gaul, they came upon the fortified town of Aventicum, the capital city for the Helvetii tribal confederation, that spread out along the western bank of the frigid Rhone River that flowed from high in the Transalpine Gaul (Swiss Alps) mountains as it meandered across the valley.

Hannibal was pleased when an advanced detachment of Helvetii soldiers rode out to the army and informed him that the Helvetii people welcomed him as a liberator from Roman oppression and offered their alliance, as well as the bounty of their rich harvest of grains, vegetables, and fruits. They were also willing to sell or trade for their sheep, cattle, and pigs, as well. While crossing the valley approaching Helvetii, Hannibal gave strict orders to all his officers that no harm was to come to the people, their property, or their lands. He knew that one day he might need these Gauls as allies.

Hannibal was grateful for the support the Helvetii so freely offered, but he also knew that their loyalty could be fleeting and unreliable, so he dispatched a second rear guard of ten thousand infantry and slingers under the command of his brother Mago. Their task was to protect the supply wagons as they descended from the Pyrenees down into Gaul.

As the Gaul spies in New Carthage predicted, crossing the Rhone was a treacherous undertaking. The stretch of the Rhone near Aventicum was no more than four-hundred feet across to the other bank but melting snow had caused it to overflow into lower areas. It was deep, swift, and freezing cold. The only bridge had been washed away during the early floods and the villagers, who were not in any hurry to go anywhere in particular, had not bothered to repair it, choosing to wait until summer to do so when the river would be much lower.

The Helvetii chieftain allowed a limited number of trees to be cut, so the army could only build a few barges. A cavalry officer managed to coax his horse to swim across the rapid current, trailing a long, thick rope behind him to the opposite shore to pull the barges across.

After a week of backbreaking, back-and-forth efforts to transport his army across the Rhone, Hannibal grew impatient and ordered the men to get across any way they could, as fast as possible. Those with horses managed best. The strong Arabians struggled against the currents, but all made the crossing. The mules did as well, also, but many of the oxen were lost. Fortunately for other livestock they got to ride across on the barges.

Titus knew from his time in the rivers of Carthage with Surus she was not afraid of moving water, and she could swim across this river. She hoisted him and then Cleopatra on her back. He clung to a tether around her neck and Cleopatra clung to him, her arms pressed tight around his waist with hands tightly clinging to his belt.

The other mahouts and their elephants watched with trepidation as Titus convinced Surus to enter the fast-moving water. The freezing cold caught her by surprise. One front leg dangled in the air as she was reluctant to lower it, but Titus' whispers convinced her to keep moving.

"I cannot swim in such water," Cleopatra whispered in a shaky voice as she clung to him even tighter.

"Do not worry," he said as he touched her right leg reassuringly. "Surus can swim for the both of us."

"Keep going," Hasdrubal shouted encouragement to them. "Follow as soon as they are clear," he ordered the other mahouts.

The men looked from him to the river. It was evident they were not confident of their prospects. The twenty Indian elephants that joined the march in New Carthage were experienced swimmers, but the sixteen other African elephants came from northern Numidia and Mauretania, both being desert regions. Swimming was not something that came natural to them.

On Hasdrubal's signal, Titus murmured to Surus to move into

the river. Without further hesitation, she stepped into the deep water, held her trunk high as only the top of her head was clear of the water, and began to swim. The water quickly reached Titus' knees. Cleopatra pulled her legs up to her chest to keep them out of the freezing water and squeezed Titus' chest so hard he felt he would pass out.

As big and powerful as Surus was it proved to be a struggle for her to swim straight across to the other side. She was swept downstream a few yards but was able to touch the bottom and she eventually hauled herself up the opposite bank, as a cascade of water flowed off her. She snorted what water had gone up her trunk then raised and sniffed at the two to check that they were still secure.

Titus turned Surus to face the village and signaled to the others to begin crossing. The smaller, lighter Indian elephants and their mahouts went first, one after the other. The elephants trumpeted their displeasure at the freezing water, being used to the warmer waters of India. The passage went well, and all were soon grazing in the long grass on the other side of the river.

The first African elephant refused to enter the water and no matter how much pleading and coaxing its mahout did it could only stare in fear at the river as it planted its front feet in the mud.

Hasdrubal nodded toward two men who had long poles with sharp metal tips called bullhooks. They stepped behind the balking elephant and jabbed at its back legs. The elephant bellowed and leapt forward, plunging into the frigid water, and swam for its life.

It was a big, strong, young bull and its powerful legs soon brought it to the other side.

Most of the others, though, were young cows who were terrified but under the men's prodding they reluctantly moved into the river. By the time they reached the center of the river, being poor swimmers, they were exhausted. Being shorter than Surus, they could not reach the bottom, and they began to sink, and their trunks slipped beneath the surface. They panicked and the disaster was immediate as they and their mahouts were swept downstream. Only three managed to struggle to the opposite bank. All the others drowned.

Before the first day's battle with Rome had taken place, Hannibal's most powerful weapon had been reduced by twelve drowned elephants. Even more of his army would drown that day because hundreds could not swim. Many were saved only because Titus convinced Surus to re-enter the river. The young bull followed her without hesitation. Together, they stood solidly, head-to-head and trunks locked together as a breakwater in the center so that another rope that was stretched across could serve as a lifeline. All the while, the few barges were being used downstream to bring over the wagons and supplies, as well as the mules and livestock.

More than thirteen hundred men, fourteen children and five women drowned.

This was not a good beginning. Are the gods against me? How many more would die before they met their hated enemy? Hannibal wondered.

Chapter Eighteen

The chieftain agreed to let some of his young men lead Hannibal the four hundred thirty-five miles across Gaul to the foothills and then across the Alps. So far, the march that began at the Ebro River and across the Pyrenees took fourteen days to travel two hundred miles. The cost had been high. Hannibal especially regretted losing so many of the elephants so early in the campaign. While men could be replaced, elephants could not, he reasoned.

He must have known from the beginning Rome's strategy would be one of attrition. He could not know, though, that the war would drag on for seventeen years, and that his rear supply route would be under constant attack because Scipio had retaken New Carthage. He would soon realize that Rome's end game was apparently to have just one more man standing than Hannibal at the end of the day.

Carthage was on the losing side of this tactic because Rome could replenish supplies and men indefinitely, where as Carthage was powerless to support Hannibal either by sea because of the Roman blockade across the Mediterranean or overland because New Carthage was now in Roman hands and the Celtic tribes in Rome's pay conducted unrelenting attacks on the supply wagons.

When they reached the trailhead of the Col de la Traversette at the foot of the Cottian Alps, located in the southwestern part of the mountain range, they could see two towns founded by Phoenicia, Crissolo and Abries. Having sent scouts ahead, Hannibal knew it would be extremely cold, and the air would be difficult to breathe at the higher altitudes of the Alps. He had no way of knowing how high they must climb (the altimeter would not be invented for over two thousand years, but it would have informed him they would have to ascend over nine thousand, six-hundred feet), or how long the march would take. He had been informed that a small party of men had crossed the same route he intended to use by horse in eight days. Out of the ninety-thousand infantry, five-thousand cavalry, the army had been cut down to seventy-thousand, and the cavalry to four thousand.

After half a day's travel the column was stretched out for miles along the narrow, twisting passage not much wider than a trail frequented by herds of ibex and chamois. With thousands of strong men and elephants at his disposal Hannibal made quick progress in clearing rock falls and cutting into the mountain to widen the path when necessary to accommodate the wagons. Scouts would continually report back to him about potential obstructions.

The first death came suddenly. A single boulder plummeted from above and smashed through a wagon full of grain, killing the driver instantly. There was no time or place to bury him, so with little ceremony his body was tossed over the edge of the steep cliff. Curious onlookers watched it fall thousands of feet until it disappeared in the clouds below.

The next day more died. Many more.

On that day, the earth seemed to rise up from itself. Animals and humans alike panicked. Women and children cried and screamed. Mules, horses, and elephants screamed in their fashion. With a solid rock wall climbing hundreds of feet above them to their right and a bottomless drop off to their left there was no place they could go and no shelter from the terror that rained down on them.

A monstrous avalanche, seemingly triggered by the incessant thrumming of hooves and the mournful cries of the wind, tumbled down the mountainside, engulfing hundreds streaming along the narrow trail in a torrent of ice and rock. The screams of humans and animals were sharp and brief, snuffed out like a flickering candle flame.

The avalanche struck with the suddenness of a lightning strike. Hannibal likened it to the powerful sneeze from the Greek mountain god Ourea, child of Gaea, the goddess of the earth. Luckily, he was well clear of the disaster, and by happenstance Titus, Cleopatra and Surus were near him, but many others were not so fortunate.

The mountain roared.

A billowing sheet of white mist that was deep, smother snow descended like a tidal wave swallowing men and animals whole. Screams, raw and desperate, were cut short, engulfed by the icy maw.

Titus and Cleopatra huddled beneath Surus who stood like a rocky outcrop, clinging to each other. Just feet away from them the world dissolved into a chaotic maelstrom of crashing ice, splintering wood, and the deafening silence of the fallen.

When the avalanche finally coughed itself out, leaving behind a desolate tableau of white, a choked sob escaped Cleopatra's lips. Tears, frozen before they could fall, traced icy tracks down her face. Thousands of feet below, the valley floor, once teeming with life, was now a graveyard of shattered dreams and broken bodies. The silence, thick and suffocating, pressed down upon those who were fortunate to have clung to the thin ribbon of a trail around the mountain. They listened to the whimpers of the wounded and the frantic moans of the dying.

The mountain rumbled again, and the survivors looked up with fear. But the mountain held its breath, a pregnant pause as Hannibal rode past a group of soldiers already pulling the debris from the avalanche off some of those who were buried.

One of those half buried was Polybius. His uncle Callisthones had been complaining to his nephew and cursing only a moment before about the frigid wind that gnawed at his exposed ears and legs. The next moment the world dissolved into a maelstrom of ice and screeching rock. The earth heaved beneath their feet, the ground tilting at an impossible angle, and then, they were airborne, tumbling head over heels in a torrent of frozen chaos.

Polybius' landing was pure agony of bone crunching against stone. Gasping for breath, he lay pinned beneath a jagged shard of ice, his vision swimming with stars. Panic, cold and a metallic taste clawed at his throat. Then, amidst the echoes of falling debris and the distant cries of terrified men and women, and the agonizing screams of the injured, there was a heart-wrenching cry of dying elephants. He recognized one in particular, a young female that he had come to know, along with the young mahout, who cared for her.

"Polybius!" Callisthones shouted frantically. His grizzled face carved with a desperate fear that mirrored Polybius' own. Callisthones' burly arms strained against the weight of a fallen boulder and dug frantically at the ice, chipping away at Polybius' icy prison. Every groan, every curse, was a prayer against the encroaching silence.

Finally, with a raw cry of exertion, Callisthones freed Polybius' leg. He was free, his limbs numb from the cold and lack of circulation. He found himself cradled in his uncle's embrace.

"Thought I lost you, nephew," Callisthones rasped, tears freezing on his weathered cheeks. Polybius was overwhelmed by a surge of relief and gratitude as he squeezed Callisthones' arm, the unspoken words hanging heavy between them.

Around them, the scene was one of unimaginable carnage. Men, once vibrant and alive, were now silent statues buried under tons of snow and rock. The cries of the wounded mingled with the mournful calls of alpine eagles, creating a symphony of despair. Hannibal, his face gaunt and etched with pain, surveyed the wreckage, his eyes hard with the cold grip of command. He knew they could not afford to dwell on the dead. The living demanded his attention, their survival his only duty.

He rallied his scattered men, their voices cracking with grief and exhaustion. Each step was a battle against the gnawing cold and the weight of their loss. Some stumbled, surrendering to the icy embrace of the mountains, their spirits extinguished. Others, fueled by a raw, primal rage, pushed on, their eyes burning with a thirst for vengeance against the unforgiving mountain gods that had claimed their comrades.

Titus steered Surus around the narrow path and together with the young bull elephant that someone had named Behemoth after the Jewish monster that supposedly lived east of the Garden of Eden, they labored through the day, the night and into the next day along with thousands of men to clear the path. They had no machinery or mechanization of any kind.

The men, their hearts still numb from the tragedy, answered Hannibal's call. Fueled by grief and a desperate hope, they formed a living chain, their hands calloused and raw, their backs bent under the weight of the fallen ice. The elephants became battering rams, their mighty trunks clearing boulders and dislodging frozen rubble.

Titus' muscles screamed in protest, joined the human chain, his hands clenched around a block of ice. Next to him, Cleopatra, her face streaked with soot and tears, dug with the ferocity of a cornered tigress. Hours bled into days, the sun a pale, indifferent orb in the endless grey sky. Every groan of shifting ice threatened to reignite the avalanche; every frostbitten finger lost a testament to their ordeal.

But just as despair threatened to engulf them, a sliver of hope emerged. The path, choked with debris, began to reveal its rocky spine. The cheers that erupted with each unearthed boulder carried the echoes of the fallen comrades, their sacrifice paving the way for continued life.

Finally, after what seemed like an eternity, the blockage yielded. The path ahead, though scarred, and treacherous, was passable. The army, though horribly diminished in numbers, was wary yet unbroken, as they stumbled through, their faces turned towards the promise of sun-drenched valleys and war with their hated enemy.

Hannibal, his once-proud crimson cloak clung to him like a shroud, urged them onward. His spirit, though tested, remained as if tempered steel. He knew their survival hinged on reaching the plains of Italia before winter's final blow. The Gauls, their eyes flickering with an unsettling mixture of fear and respect, guided them along treacherous paths.

Hannibal rallied his scattered men, their voices cracking with grief and exhaustion. Each step was a battle against the gnawing cold and the weight of their loss. Some stumbled, surrendering to the icy embrace of the mountains, their spirits extinguished like flickering candle flames. Others, fueled by a desperate rage, pushed on, eyes burning with a thirst for surviving one more day and to leave the unforgiving mountains that had claimed their comrades.

The severely injured and dying were left behind to be cared for by the healers and volunteers who, once the injured were able to travel, would take them back to New Carthage. There were over thirty-five hundred who would begin the journey back. Nearly half would die in the mountains from their injuries. Over two hundred would be killed as the diminishing band of survivors fought their way back to New Carthage through the Celtic tribes loyal to Rome.

Polybius and Callisthones were among those who returned and

relayed the tale of horror that had befallen the army that would one day be the genesis of Polybius' *The Histories*. Polybius would eventually return to Greece to begin his forty-volume collection of Hannibal's unprecedented march against Rome. Callisthones would perish at sea three years later aboard a Carthaginian blockade runner sunk by a Roman warship.

Though Cleopatra considered herself a warrior, she was a woman first, whose heart went out to those who were left behind as others were flung into space to fall to their deaths. Field doctors or *medici* and healers, called *rhizotomiki* worked together to set up a triage nearby where the wounded and dying were cared for. Wounds were cleaned as well as possible and bandages were applied. Broken bones were set. There were several amputations of arms and legs. The screams were unending. Cleopatra was everywhere, helping with calming children and comforting the injured as best as she could.

Besides Surus and Behemoth there were only twelve others still able to stand against the gale winds and snow. Four fell to their knees, their heads held up by their tusks. The mahouts tried their best to keep their elephants warm with fires around them but once the elephants went down on their chests it was only a matter of time before they would die from asphyxiation.

The Alps, once imagined a shortcut across continents, now loomed as a leviathan, its icy breath rasping against the Carthaginians' throats. The Gauls, their promises of swift passage echoed in Hannibal's mind as emptily as the wind, as his army huddled behind flickering fires that offered little comfort. The army, once a vibrant tapestry of men and beasts, was now a procession of ghosts, their faces etched with frostbite and despair.

Every day his army dwindled by one or two and then tens and twenties. Frostbite was unknown to most who had grown up in desert climates. More died from frostbite's frigged breath than any previous enemy weapons.

At over seven-thousand feet altitude, the sun is a pale, indifferent orb in the endless grey sky. At over seven-thousand, two hundred feet, men who had lived their entire lives at or below sea level had difficulty breathing and moving. Fortunately, the elephants' lack of a plural cavity, the fluid-filled space between the two membranes that gave them unique respiratory systems, allowed them to easily breathe at high altitudes. Whereas the horses, mules and oxen had difficulty carrying supplies and riders, the elephants seemed energetic by comparison.

But the elephants suffered as did the other animals as feed became scarce. The army faired better, living off the flesh of the animals as they died. Because the alpine forests in the Alps often grew as high as eight-thousand feet, there was sufficient wood for cooking fires and warmth, when the icy, gale-force winds let up, which was not often at first.

Their once proud, colorful attire hung in rags, offering scant protection against the elements. Yet, they soldiered on, driven by a flicker of hope, a stubborn refusal to yield to the mountain's will.

Hannibal was a man of stark contradictions that became more evident during the crossing. Renowned for his ruthless battlefield tactics, he simultaneously displayed deep affection for his family and his soldiers. Through shared hardships, he led the army across the Alps into Italia in just sixteen days.

It was costly, though.

Finally, after two weeks of what seemed like an eternity, the Alps coughed up the battered Carthaginian army onto the plains of the Po Valley into an area known as Cisalpine Gaul, which is now northern Italy. Emerging from the icy maw of the mountains, they stumbled into the sun-drenched valleys, their eyes blinking at the unfamiliar brightness. The sight of green grass, a whisper of spring in the air, brought tears to many weather-beaten faces.

Hannibal's army of over ninety-four thousand infantry and twelve-thousand cavalry had dwindled down to thirty-thousand infantry and six-thousand cavalry. The physical remains of thousands of men and animals were never to be discovered over two-thousand, two hundred years following Hannibal's great march to Italia.

Only in the year 2024 did scientist finally discover evidence along the trail that elephants once grazed there and left droppings along the way.

Fortunately, some thirty-thousand Gallic mercenaries eager to fight against Rome joined the ragged ranks of his army. Their knowledge of the local terrain was crucial to Hannibal's success in the early campaign in Italia. They were fierce fighters whose favorite weapon was the long sword, which required elbow room, as it were, so they preferred to fight as individuals rather than in close ranks as did the Romans and Carthaginians. And there was no mistaking them on the battlefield as they preferred to fight naked or dressed in outlandish armor so as to stand out in a display of heroism.

As terrifying as the Gauls were as individual warriors on the battlefield, Hannibal's ruthlessness was renowned even among them. He often found it necessary to be unmerciful in all aspects of war to the point of utter annihilation of entire societies when it came to fighting more powerful enemies. In this, he was no different than the Babylonians, Macedonians, Persians, Spartans, or the Romans before him. All erased societies from existence through war and assimilation.

To maintain the loyalty of his polyglot, or multilingual army, composed of Carthaginians, Numidians, Hispanics, Gauls, and the lone Syrian girl Cleopatra, he employed a policy of calculated terror. He would not order his army to do anything he was not willing to do himself, and always led the battles from the front lines, often including his brothers Hasdrubal and Mago, as well as his nephew Hanno. He famously had Roman prisoners slaughtered in sight of their own city, a display of power aimed at breaking their countrymen's morale.

Yet, beneath his ruthless exterior, Hannibal was a man capable of rare tenderness. His bond with his younger brother Hasdrubal was one of deep love and mutual respect. Eleven years into the war when Hasdrubal was killed as he charged alone at the Roman enemy after his own armies had been defeated during the Battle of Metaurus, Hannibal could not be consoled. Historians recorded that he built a pyre the size of a city and mourned his brother for days, a stark contrast to the stoic image he projected towards his troops.

Even as they licked their wounds, a tremor of excitement ran through the ranks. Rome, the enemy they had come so far to destroy, was within reach. The air buzzed with whispers of battle, of vengeance, and of a dream, a flickering ember refusing to be extinguished. The Alps, though they had taken a heavy toll, had not quelled the Carthaginian spirit. They had emerged, bloodied but not broken, ready to face the Romans on their own soil.

Chapter Nineteen

The crossing of the Alps was not just a physical feat; it was a baptism of fire that by the time the Carthaginians spilled out of the mountains they were a formidable fighting force. They were bloodied and beaten but they were tempered by the icy winds and an unforgiving terrain and nature's fury. As the first chapter on the Alps closed, the second chapter of their Italia campaign was opening, the echoes of the avalanche, the mournful cries of the wind, and the terrible screams of their fallen comrades would forever be etched in their memories. They had paid a heavy price in one of the most audacious military gambles before and since.

The morning mist hung low over the Po plains, shrouding the land in a veil of mystery as the first rays of sunlight pierced through the fog. It had been only three months since the army left New Carthage. Though bent by tragedy and the loss of so many, the army's spirit was unbroken, and its general's resolve was unwavering.

The Roman forces, made up of two legions that included eighteen-thousand infantry, along with eighteen-hundred cavalry that disembarked were supplied by sixty warships. This formidable force was led by none other than the Consul Publius Cornelius

Scipio, the very same man Hannibal had foolishly released after he was rescued at sea.

Scipio had been tracking the movements of the Carthaginian army and was eager to confront these invaders that were daring to challenge Rome, the second time since Hannibal's father Hamilcar had done just twenty-three years before.

Scipio used the warships to transport much of his army along the coast from Massalia (modern-day Marseille) to Pisa, where he informed the Roman Senate that he intended to take command of Roman forces as he marched to the Po Valley arriving before Hannibal's army. Shortly thereafter, Roman cavalry engaged the Carthaginian's Numidian cavalry at the Ticinus River. Scipio believed this was not a battle for territory but a battle for the very soul of Rome.

As the two armies faced each other, the tension was palpable. Gaia and Micipsa were right out front where they wanted to be as the Numidian cavalry, swift and agile, stood ready, their eyes scanning the horizon for any sign of movement. The Roman cavalry, disciplined and formidable, mirrored their adversaries, their hands steady on the reins.

The silence was broken by the thunderous sound of the elephants. In the lead were the two companions Surus and Behemoth. Behind them were the fifteen other surviving elephants. Their massive forms loomed above a ground-hugging fog, instilling fear, and awe in the hearts of the Romans. None of them had ever faced elephants in battle. They had heard the tales of Alexander the Great using elephants to crush his enemies. They had not come prepared to fight such monsters.

Titus and Cleopatra stood on either side of Surus to protect her. He did not need to ride her because Surus would follow him anywhere, so he was free to fight by her side or in front of her. Cleopatra had her bow ready, a sword on her hip and a small shield strapped to her back; Titus had his sling and a bag full of stones, as well as sword and shield on his back. Both wore leather and metal chest armor and high leather boots, as well as bronze Iberian helmets.

To gain the highest ground on the flat river plain to direct the battle, Hannibal stood in a howdah or basket made of a wood frame with reinforced leather on Surus' back. She wore her full coat of heavy leather and padding over her entire body, in addition to a custom-made leather helmet to protect her head. To make her even more lethal the bronze points were again added to her tusks. In a nod to ancient-times psychological warfare, she was fitted with bells to create noise to intimidate the enemy. Because Titus was not on her back, in addition to carrying Hannibal Surus was also able to carry three archers to protect him and to fire at the enemy as the elephant rumbled like a four-legged tank through the enemy.

Titus took several stones from his bag and fitted one into the sling. He focused on the line of enemy cavalry across the field and let the sling hang at his side. He was not worried about dying. He really had no understanding of death even though he had witnessed it numerous times since leaving Carthage. The way he looked at death was that the person who died was simply gone. He had no concept of an afterlife or given any thought to what it meant to die. He did, though, feel some anxiety about Surus' and Cleopatra's safety. He may not understand death, but he understood pain, and he did not want either of them to suffer pain. He was determined to do everything in his power to prevent pain from being inflicted on them. He glanced over at Cleopatra, and she smiled bravely back at him and raised her bow.

One of the archers with Hannibal raised a flag over his head and then brought it down, signaling the charge. The Numidian cavalry surged forward, a wave of speed and ferocity, the tips of their arrows glinting in the sunlight. Gaia and Micipsa were at the head of the charge, bellowing a bloodthirsty challenge toward the hated Romans. The Roman cavalry responded in kind, their own charge a testament to their discipline and courage.

The clash was monumental as the sound of metal-on-metal, horse-flesh-on-horse flesh echoed across the plains. The Numidians, with their superior maneuverability in riding bareback, and with no armor eliminated the weight that allowed them to dart in and out of the Roman formations, firing arrows at point-blank distance, causing chaos and confusion. Micipsa put one arrow into the chest of a high-ranking legionnaire. He hoped it was Scipio. It was not.

Scipio rode at the head of his cavalry. He was a veteran of countless wars against countless enemies. He fought valiantly, his sword cutting through the air with precision, cutting down one Numidian after another.

"Stay firm, men of Rome!" he shouted above the din of battle. "For every home, for every hearth, for the glory of Rome!"

The battle was evenly matched—for the opening round, but the elephants were the true game-changers. Twin Titans Surus and Behemoth, ahead of the phalanx of war elephants charged through the Romans, terrifying their horses, and trampling any man or horse that fell beneath them. Their massive bodies crashed through the Roman lines, trampling, and scattering the soldiers like leaves in a storm. Hannibal watched from his perch atop Surus, directing the battle with signal flags.

"Push them back!" he commanded, his voice carrying over the sounds of war. "Let the might of Carthage be felt!"

Titus let fly with his sling and struck a Roman officer between the eyes. The man was dead before he flipped backwards off his horse. Another Roman charged at Titus to run him down when an arrow through his throat flung him off to be trampled by Surus. Titus glanced back to see Cleopatra notching another arrow and letting it fly in one smooth motion.

Suddenly Roman infantry appeared from behind the cavalry. They charged at the Numidians but were no match for the elephants. This was their first encounter with elephants, and they did not know how to fight them. A few fired arrows at the elephants but the heavy armor deflected them. When the elephants bellowed their terrifying war cries mingled with the bells each carried the Romans began to run.

The battle raged on; the outcome uncertain. The Romans, though taken aback by the elephants, regrouped, and fought with renewed vigor. Scipio, wounded but undeterred, rallied his men, leading them in a countercharge that pushed the Numidians back.

The battlefield became a tapestry of violence and bravery, each side giving as good as they got. The dialogue of war spoken by both armies in the language of iron and blood, was a conversation punctuated by the mournful cries of the fallen and the shouts of the living.

Titus was out of stones and Cleopatra was out of arrows. They came together in front of Surus and Behemoth with swords drawn and shields up. A dozen Romans rushed towards them. Cleopatra was skilled and fearsome, but she was diminutive compared to some of the burly Roman veterans. Muscle mass was everything and they were intent on killing her with as little effort as possible. She and Titus stood back-to-back fighting toe-to-toe against the enemy.

A sword slash slipped past Titus' shield and cut him across the chest. Cleopatra whirled around and cut the Roman down as Titus slipped to one knee, bleeding heavily. Behind them Surus smelled his blood and screamed, lowered her massive head so the tusks were aimed at the group of Romans. She ripped back and forth through their ranks with the bronze-tipped tusks like a scythe, cutting all of them down, as wheat, then trampling them into the mud.

Cleopatra helped him to his feet, handing him his sword.

"Can you still fight?" Hannibal shouted down to them.

They looked up at him. "Yes, general," they shouted in unison.

He grinned at them. "We will be victorious before the end of day," Hannibal said confidently.

They turned to the sound of horses charging at them to see Scipio headed at them with his sword prepared to cut Cleopatra down. Titus jumped in front of the charging horse and slammed his shield in the animal's chest, causing it to tumble head-first, throwing Scipio over its head. The horse struggled to its feet as Scipio drew his sword again. Just as it looked like he would cut through Cleopatra, an arrow pierced his armor in his lower chest, and he fell back.

Cleopatra was determined to finish the job and stepped toward him with her sword raised for the killing blow. She was suddenly blocked by another horse as the rider, Scipio's sixteen-year-old son leapt to the ground and fended her off until his father could regain his feet. The boy fought so fiercely he drove Cleopatra back as his father mounted the horse, then he turned back and jumped onto the horse behind his father and rode away.

Hannibal watched amazed as the fight between Cleopatra and the Roman boy unfolded. When the boy rode away with his father, Hannibal held up a hand to stop one of the archers from firing at them. He recognized Scipio and his son. He admired both for their bravery. For a second time Hannibal spared the Roman general—and this time his son. He would regret his decision.

Chapter Twenty

While Hannibal was busy routing the Roman army, the Roman navy was experiencing more success in its fight against the Carthaginian maritime forces. The rising sun cast a crimson hue over the waters surrounding Lilybaeum, a small coastal town located in western Sicily. The Roman fleet, commanded by Gaius Atilius Regulus, had been preparing for this moment for weeks. The men in the fleet waited for Regulus' command with anticipation.

"Ready the ballistae!" barked Regulus, his voice cutting through the morning stillness. His second-in-command, a seasoned veteran named Alexander Tiberius Marcellus nodded and relayed the orders to the crew. On the deck of the lead ship, mariners scurried to their battle stations loading the massive siege engines with deadly projectiles made from the mysterious incendiary known as Greek Fire that was impossible to extinguish even in water. The Carthaginian fleet was in sight, their sails billowing in the wind as they approached.

"Today, the enemy is ours," Regulus proclaimed, his eyes fixed on the enemy ships. "We fight, we live, we die for Rome."

"We fight, we live, we die for Rome!" echoed the mariners and soldiers in unison, their morale bolstered by their commander's fervor.

The first volley of flaming missiles launched from the Roman ballistae arched gracefully through the air trailing black smoke and flames before crashing into the nearest Carthaginian galley with devastating force. Wood splintered, and cries of agony rose above the sound of battle as the vessel exploded in flames.

Amidst the chaos, a young Roman officer Gaius Fabricius Luscinus clutched his gladius or short sword tightly. He was nineteen and this was his first battle, and his heart pounded in his chest like a drum. Beside him stood his childhood friend, Marius Acilius Glabrio, who offered a reassuring nod.

"We stand or die together, brother," Marius said, his voice steady despite the turmoil around them.

Suddenly, the two fleets collided. Thousands of oars were instantly splintered on both sides as bronze-covered bows crashed through them. Screams could be heard inside the hulls from the rowers. Glabrio and Fabricius leaped through flames onto a Carthaginian ship, their blades slashing through flesh.

"Push them back!" Glabrio shouted as he blocked a blow from a Carthaginian defender. Fabricius fought fiercely at his side, men falling at their feet their teamwork a testament to years of training.

The Carthaginian fleet commander signaled for his ships to break away from the Romans to fight another day. Regulus was having none of it. He had the enemy in his clutches and was determined to destroy the entire fleet as he maneuvered his ships to encircle them, cutting off their escape. His focus was capturing the flagship and either capturing or killing the commander, a man who had alluded capture before.

As the Roman soldiers lowered the ramp between the ships they surged forward, boarding the enemy flagship. The fight was brutal and relentless. Finally, after what seemed like an eternity, the Carthaginian admiral was wounded but alive, barely, when he was taken captive. When the Carthaginian crew saw their admiral taken prisoner, they ceased fighting and threw down their weapons. They should have kept fighting because the Romans were not about to be bothered with keeping prisoners alive. Normally, the prisoners would have been transported to the slave markets but the hatred between Rome and Carthage was so great that destruction was the order of the day.

As the sounds of battle ebbed the two young officers stood side by side on the deck of the captured flagship, their armor stained with the blood of their sworn enemies.

"Victory," Fabricius breathed, a mixture of exhaustion and elation in his voice.

"For Rome," Glabrio completed the war chant.

The Battle of Lilybaeum would be one of the pivotal moments in the war. With a standing blockade of the Italia and Hispania ports, it would prove to be impossible to supply Hannibal's army for the remainder of the war, forcing him to adapt by recruiting more fighters from the local populations while simultaneously pillaging every city and farm in his path.

By the end of 218 BC Hannibal had experienced victories in minor skirmishes at Ticinus and Trebia. The new year brought his first two major victories at the Battle of Trasimene and the Battle of Ager Falernus within weeks of one another. Titus, Cleopatra, Surus, and the two Namibian brothers Micipsa and Gaia were there to take part in both.

On June 21, 217 BC Hannibal rode at the head of his army on the back of Surus as Titus and Cleopatra walked on either side of her while they marched across the Apennines Mountains along the length of the Italia peninsula. The army had been continually moving for more than a year, living off the land or by what they could pillage from the towns they leveled. Hannibal, like Alexander the Great, who died one hundred six years before, never suffered a severe injury from battle but he was brought low by an infection from a waterborne organism while marching through the Arno River lowland marshes, in the Tuscany region of central Italia.

Hannibal was not able to stop long enough to allow the healers time to treat the eye and the infection grew steadily worse over the ensuing months and by the time he was about to lead his army into the most significant battle of what would be a protracted war of seventeen years, he was blind in his right eye. If nothing else, though, Hannibal was resilient, even with one eye.

Initially, his spatial awareness or the ability to determine the relationship between objects to himself, and depth of perception, two crucial attributes for any military commander, were affected.

Early on this caused him to be more irritable than usual and he was often anxious. But he was primarily a battle-tested warrior and a brilliant tactician. He adapted quickly by shifting his cognitive capabilities to his senses of smell, touch, and hearing. He also put more trust in his officers and those closest to him.

He especially depended on the two teenagers who walked beside the magnificent Surus, as well as their bravery and fighting skills in protecting her, and by extension himself. He thought it curious that he did not know who was more important to them, himself or Surus.

Surus, surely, he thought. *It did not matter. They had saved the elephant and himself more than once.*

Covered in lush forest lands ringing broad grasslands, the highest peak in the Apennine Mountains was Corno Grande at nine-thousand five hundred fifty-four feet. This mountain range was home to two of the fiercest predators, the Marsican brown bear and the Italian wolf.

Using loyal Gaul scouts, Hannibal was already familiar with the terrain where he planned to ambush the army led by Consul Gaius Flaminius. Thanks to the scouts Hannibal knew when Flaminius was leaving Arretium and the planned route he would take to the valley where Lake Trasimene was located. The day before Flaminius' legionnaires were to arrive Hannibal arranged his heavy infantry and archers in the hills around the lake and the cavalry and light infantry to the eastern end of the valley to block any possible Roman retreat.

As Flaminius led his men through the morning fog into the trap, Hannibal stood in the basket on top of Surus where he could plainly see them. His signal was relayed along the protracted line of infantry and a moment later they ran down the hills while the Numidian cavalry circled around behind the Romans, cutting them off from the entrance to the valley as they charged into their ranks.

The canyon was a narrow passage through the rugged terrain, a natural choke point that the Roman legion had hoped to use to their advantage. The Numidian cavalry had been harrying the Roman flanks for days, but now they were out for blood.

The Romans advanced, their shields interlocked, spears at the ready. The Numidians, led by the fearless Gaia and the cunning Micipsa, had been watching from the high ground, their horses stamping impatiently. Now, as they charged at the hated Romans a hail of javelins killed many of the horsemen. but the Numidians were not so easily cowed. With a thunderous cry, Gaia led the charge from the left flank, his horse leaping effortlessly over the Roman shields as Gaia spun his horse around and fired arrows into the soldiers' backs. Micipsa followed, his eyes alight with the fire of battle.

The Romans were braced for impact, but the Numidians were too quick, too agile. They darted in and out of the Roman lines, their arrows cutting down soldiers. The Romans fought bravely, but they were unprepared for the ferocity and skill of their opponents.

As the skirmish wore on, the Romans' discipline and training allowed them to reform their defensive wall that the Carthaginian infantry struggled to penetrate. It seemed as though the Romans might recover and hold the line in the hope they could gain a foothold on the hillside.

The elephants and infantry were taking their toll on the right flank. On the left flank, Gaia and Micipsa rallied their men, calling out to each warrior by name, reminding them of the glory that awaited them. With renewed vigor, the Numidians attacked again, their horses running down the Romans with such force that the Roman line began to buckle.

The turning point came when Micipsa saw Surus and Behemoth break through the Roman line. With a deft maneuver, he led a contingent of cavalry through the break, attacking from the side and sowing chaos in the ranks.

Now surrounded, the Romans tried to retreat, but there was no place to retreat to. Their escape route out of the valley was cut off. Step by step, they were pushed back toward the lake. There was no way forward, and no way back.

Realizing their fate, the Romans stood their ground in the water and fought with the desperation of men who knew their time with the living was ending. One by one, they were forced back further into deeper water. Some fought and died where they stood, while many tried to swim but were weighted down with armor or could not swim and quickly disappeared below the surface.

In their home country one day in the future the skirmish in the canyon would be remembered as a testament to the courage of the Numidian people, and the names of Gaia and Micipsa would be sung by bards for generations to come. For on that day, they had faced the might of the Roman Republic and emerged triumphant, their enemies vanquished, their honor intact.

The ambush would go down in military history where an entire Roman army was destroyed. While the casualties on the Carthaginian side were around twenty-five hundred killed, more than fifteen thousand Roman soldiers, including their commander, Gaius Flaminius, were killed in battle or drowned trying to escape across the lake. It was devastating to Rome and in a panic its citizens elected Quintus Fabius Maximus Verrucosus for the second time (he was first elected in 221 BC), as the country's dictator.

Known as the *Cunctator* (Latin for procrastinator), Verrucosus' strategy, which became known as the *Fabian strategy*, in fighting against Hannibal, included avoiding decisive battles, practicing a war of attrition, indirect actions such as cutting off enemy supply lines, scorched-earth warfare, and using time as an ally.

Fortunately for Hannibal, in the initial years of fighting, he did not have to depend on supplies being brought over the Alps. Instead, he relied on foraging, seizing supplies from the countryside, and the support of local allies in Italia to sustain his army, which allowed him to keep fighting.

While the Battle of Trasimene was a significant victory for Hannibal, the war would continue for another sixteen years with new battles every few weeks. The Romans regrouped repeatedly to keep the fight coming to Hannibal. With a population of approximately ten million, not counting slaves or foreigners in Italia, the Roman army could recruit from its citizens, whereas Hannibal had to depend on the sporadic help of allies, including Galic and Celtic tribes, Macedonia, Syracuse, and the Numidian Kingdom. In later years, many of these either changed sides and joined Rome against Carthage or sued for a separate peace.

It wasn't until nine years after the beginning of the war, in 207 BC, that Hasdrubal was able to organize another army and brought reinforcements, consisting of eleven thousand eight hundred fifty Carthaginian infantry, four hundred Numidian cavalry, eighteen hundred Numidian and Moorish infantry, and twenty-one more elephants from Carthage, again crossing the Alps.

Unfortunately, his army was defeated at the Battle of the Metaurus that same year. Most of his army was annihilated, with many either captured or ran away to somehow make their way back to Carthage or, more likely, assimilate into the population.

It happened on June 22 that his army was destroyed. Knowing he could not escape and not wanting to be captured, Hasdrubal mounted his horse, held his sword in defiance, and charged at the enemy alone. He was killed in a hail of arrows and then beheaded. Later, his head was thrown into Hannibal's camp as a sign of contempt and maximum defeat. In any event, the army was prevented from joining Hannibal's forces and except for some meager attempts to support him by sea, support in Italia was totally cut off for the rest of the war.

If the loss of over twenty-thousand men and most of his elephants was not bad enough, Hannibal's decision not to march on Rome was a strategic misstep of major proportions. Instead, he involved his army in several skirmishes that continually whittled away at the size of his army through battles and the harsh conditions, which was the very definition of the Roman tactic of conducting a war of attrition.

While the Roman's strategy called for hit-and-run tactics and avoiding major battles, Hannibal's army was marching headlong through hundreds of miles of hostile territories and its men were being picked off in ever-increasing numbers.

Like a plague of locusts, his army stripped clean the lands they passed through, further increasing their enemies as they reduced their numbers for the lack of food and vital war supplies. By the time the Battle of Ager Falernus took place, the army had been reduced to about four thousand infantry, two thousand cavalry, two thousand camp followers, and eight elephants.

Three months after the brilliant defeat of Roman forces at the battle at Lake Trasimene took place, Hannibal's army marched the one hundred twenty-five miles to the area near Mount Callicula, where he was to meet Verrucosus' army for the first time.

The battle was fought in the district of Falernum, a fertile river valley surrounded by mountains. Again, Hannibal's knowledge of the terrain provided him with the tactical advantage.

Even though his army was vastly outnumbered by the Romans, again, he was able to position his soldiers on high ground, giving him the strategic advantage.

Once again, Titus and Cleopatra were alongside Surus as she, along with Behemoth and the other six elephants charged at the Romans. This time, though, the Romans did not run from the elephants. Instead, they launched heavy spears and projectiles with their *onagers* or catapults at the elephants and infantry. Heavy spears killed two of the elephants. When they fell several Carthaginian soldiers were crushed. The Romans purposefully aimed at killing the mahouts. They had learned by killing them the elephants would panic. That is what happened when four of the mahouts fell. Their elephants immediately turned and ran back through their own forces, killing more Carthaginians.

Without the mahouts, the elephants were crazed and could not be brought under control, so the Carthaginians were forced to kill the four. Now, only Surus and Behemoth were left to continue forward as Cleopatra protected them both from the Roman infantry with her unerring accuracy as her arrows took down one Roman after another. Titus fought by her side, protecting her with his shield as he cut down any Roman who drew near them.

Behind them Surus and Behemoth slashed to their left and right with their bronze-covered tusks at any Roman who tried to slip behind the two young warriors. The surviving Romans took note of the two. They would remember them.

Titus and Cleopatra could not protect the elephants from the onagers, though. A long, sharp spear launched from one of the machines sliced through the leather armor and along Surus' side, causing a long slash. Then a rock struck her in the head and blood flowed down her face, into her eyes and along her trunk. Another, larger rock hit her right tusk, breaking off two feet of it. She bellowed in pain and shook her head furiously, nearly throwing off Hannibal and the archers on her back.

Titus looked back at his beloved Surus. He knew she was in pain but there was nothing he could do for her at that moment. If they

survived, he thought, he would do what he could to relieve her pain. But for now, they must continue to fight.

The battle spread across open ground covered in tall grass. A flaming projectile hurled from the Roman side skidded through the dry grass setting it afire. The blaze burst across the field catching Romans and Carthaginians in its fury. Men were torn between fighting or fleeing. Many feared the nearby swamp as much as they did the fire. Many could not outrun the flames and died horribly. Others made it to the forest.

Hannibal and his men abandoned Surus when she became enraged in the pain from her broken tusk. Titus stood before her and with his soothing voice calmed her to the point he could guide her away from the flames.

"We need to go into the swamp," he told Cleopatra. The girl was skeptical but trusted Titus.

"Will she go?" she asked.

"She knows the water," he said. "You saw she was unafraid of the river."

"What if the Romans go there?"

"They are running away from it," he said, nodding in the direction of the fleeing Romans. "She needs to heal and rest."

She nodded in silent agreement, and they headed into the swamp.

Chapter Twenty-One

Titus and Cleopatra led Surus deep into the swamp. Not knowing where else to go, Behemoth and his mahout, called Ahirom, had joined them. There, in the quiet of the wetlands, Titus tended to Surus' wounds. He removed the armor and cleaned the long, deep gash on her side and her head with care, his hands steady despite the exhaustion that weighed on him. Cleopatra gathered herbs and plants known for their healing properties, applying poultices to the wounds and the end of the broken tusk. Ahirom made a clearing, gathered wood for a fire and looked for edible plants and caught a few small frogs and fish.

As night fell, Titus and Cleopatra huddled together near the small fire. Ahirom sat across the fire from them. The elephants leaned against one another nearby, their bond forged in the crucible of battle. Surus' wounds would heal in time, and they would rejoin Hannibal's forces, but for now, they had each other. In the darkness of the swamp, they found solace in the knowledge that they had survived, that they had fought not just for Carthage or for Syria, but for the unspoken promises of friendship, and possibly something more.

And so, as the first light of dawn touched the horizon, they rested, their spirits unbroken, their resolve unwavering. The battle of the field of tall grass would be remembered, not for its victors or its vanquished, but for the courage of a Carthaginian teenager, a Syrian girl, and an elephant named Surus, who together faced the flames of war and emerged triumphant.

Weeks later they emerged from the swamp and found the remnants of Hannibal's army had set up camp in the forest surrounding the clearing that had burned. The dead had been cremated in a huge funeral pyre, and the wounded were being cared for by the physicians and healers.

Because they could not be cared for or guarded, the surviving Romans had been put to the sword. The air was thick with the scent of pine and the smoke. Surus and Behemoth grazed peacefully nearby, the only surviving elephants of the original thirty-seven.

Gaia and Micipsa had found them and were sharing tales of the battle as they experienced it. Despite the recent horrors the brothers' spirits were unbroken as they reveled in the telling of how they charged into the Roman ranks. The camaraderie between the two with Titus and Cleopatra was a beacon of light in the shadow of war.

Later, with full bellies and the warmth of the fire the boys slept. Cleopatra was restless and decided to walk around the camp, lost in her thoughts, consumed by the young warrior she secretly adored. Her footsteps were soft against the earth, her presence barely a whisper in the night.

As was normal for her, she carried her bow and quiver of arrows, in addition to her long sword. She was at peace, deep in thought, and was not expecting the attack when it came suddenly and violently from behind.

Five mercenaries, including Brutus, who had fought with Titus and the brothers while still in Carthage, emerged from the shadows, grabbing her forcefully, gagging her and throwing aside her weapons. They were greedy men loyal to nothing or no one. They took what they wanted and violated women when they could, then they would murder the women when done with them.

They had been watching the beautiful young, exotic Syrian woman for months, plotting to do what they wanted with her, but when they heard of the rich bounty the Romans had placed on her and Titus, they plotted to take the two of them to the Roman camp they knew to be on the other side of the hills.

When they grabbed her Cleopatra tried to fight them, but Brutus smashed her in the face with his fist.

"Keep fighting and we will kill Titus in front of you," he threatened. She believed him and stopped struggling.

"What about the boy?" one of the mercenaries asked. "We going to take him too?"

"There are too many near him," Brutus said. "She'll have to do." He held the back of her neck and pulled her face close to his. She almost gagged at his stench.

"You even twitch and I'll snap your neck," he hissed.

She looked into his eyes. She did not fear him and only had thoughts of how she would kill him at the first opportunity.

From her grazing spot Surus watched the men lead Cleopatra away. When she saw how one of them slapped the girl in the back of the head, she trumpeted an angry call. The men turned to look at her then scurried into the trees. Surus continued her plaintiff calling until it woke Tirus and the brothers.

"Something's wrong," Titus said as he stood and saw Surus rocking back and forth anxiously. The three ran over to her. "What do you hear?" he asked her. She looked at him and then toward the trees. He followed her motion, looking for whatever was bothering her.

"What do you think it is?" Micipsa asked.

"I don't know but whatever it is it's got her upset," Titus said. "Come on, girl," he said as he led Surus toward the forest with his hand on her right tusk, as he had done hundreds of times while in Carthage as a boy. At the edge of the light from the campfires he found Cleopatra's weapons scattered in the grass.

In the forest the men heard the elephant call out. "Hurry," Brutus ordered.

"No one will come looking for the girl," a second mercenary said.

"Yes, they will," Brutus said. "I know that elephant. It has killed others and will do the same to us if we do not hurry."

"It's just an elephant," the man said.

"No, it is not just an elephant. It is a demon," Brutus said and pushed Cleopatra ahead of him.

"Find Cleopatra," Titus commanded Surus. The elephant did not hesitate and moved off toward the forest. Titus and the brothers hastily grabbed their weapons and with Surus leading the charge, they raced into the forest, their hearts pounding with a mix of fear and determination.

The chase was a maelstrom of urgency and peril. Branches whipped at their faces, and the uneven ground threatened to betray their footing at every turn. But they pressed on, driven by the bond they shared with Cleopatra and the unspoken oath they had taken to protect her.

As they closed in on the mercenaries, the forest gave way to a clearing, and the true scope of their challenge became clear. Brutus and his men were not alone; a contingent of Roman soldiers lay in wait, their swords glinting in the moonlight.

The battle that ensued was fierce and unforgiving. Titus and the brothers fought with the ferocity of lions, their blades flashing in deadly arcs through the night. Surus, a force of nature unto herself, trampled and gored any Roman or Carthaginian traitor who fell in her path, her loyalty to Cleopatra fueling her rage.

When the two forces came together, Cleopatra managed to pull herself free of Brutus' cruel grasp. She ducked as he swung his sword at her then she scampered to one side and picked up a sword dropped by one of the mercenaries who Surus had gored. Enraged, she charged at the enemy from behind as the love of her young life and his two friends fought for her.

The clash of iron and the cries of the fallen filled the air, a symphony of chaos and resolve. One by one, the kidnappers and their Roman allies fell to never rise again. The mercenaries' dreams of silver were extinguished by the unyielding spirit of the four young warriors and one enraged elephant.

Brutus lay defeated and dying at Titus' feet, his eyes wide with disbelief. The young warrior's gaze was steely, his hand unwavering as he delivered the final blow. It was a moment of triumph, but also of sorrow, for the cost of war was etched in the lines of his face.

Cleopatra dropped the bloody sword and came into Titus' arms. Finally, she knew that he knew she loved him. And she knew now that he understood what he had been feeling for her for months was love.

"Anytime you two want to go back to camp, I think we're done here," said Gaia as he grinned at his brother.

"Yes," Titus said simply as he held on to Cleopatra's hand. "Surus," he called. Surus snorted her approval and turned to lead them out of the forest.

Chapter Twenty-Two

In the fall of 215 BC, while Hasdrubal was fighting on a second front in Hispania to protect Carthaginian interests as well as Hannibal's flank, another unrelated Carthaginian general known as Hasdrubal the Bald was taking the fight against Rome to the island of Sardinia.

Hasdrubal the Bald left Carthage to reinforce Hannibal on a third front when his fleet was caught up in a storm. While his ship was wrecked off the Balearic Islands near the eastern coast of the Iberian Peninsula, two other ships from the fleet managed to anchor undetected by the Roman navy along the Italia coast where Hannibal was able to off-load a few supplies. He knew other ships in the fleet had war elephants destined for Hasdrubal the Bald's campaign and thought Surus and Titus, with all their experience in fighting the Romans over the past three years, would be assets in Sardinia.

Titus and Cleopatra were by now married, with Hannibal, himself, conducting the ceremony, and with the brothers Micipsa and Gaia witnessing the ceremony. No one, least of all Titus or Hannibal, had any doubt that Cleopatra would not only be at Titus' side as his wife but as a fellow warrior who had his back.

A few days later, with Surus and Behemoth in one of the ship's cargo holds, they were sailing for Sardinia, with a brief stop at the Balearic Islands to retrieve the marooned general. A few days later, the army landed at Tharros, where Hasdrubal the Bald met up with Sardinian forces loyal to Carthage. The next morning they began the sixty-two-mile marsh from the Sinis Peninsula on the western coast of Sardinia to Cagliari on the southern coast of the island. The veteran war elephants Surus and Behemoth led the way.

Three days later, the air was tense with anticipation as the Carthaginian forces were about to clash with the Roman legions under Praetor Titus Manlius Torquatus. What would become known as the Battle of Decimomannu was not just another fight; it was a pivotal moment that would echo the earlier struggles between Hannibal and Rome.

The purpose of this third front was hopefully to replicate Hannibal's victories in Italia. The goal was to wrest control of the strategic island that was rich in resources and a crucial point for maritime trade routes to North Africa and throughout the Mediterranean, as well as a Roman navy's homeport.

As the Carthaginian army prepared for battle, there was a palpable sense of unity among the diverse groups of Hannibal's veterans. The Libyan infantry, known for their steadfastness, took their position at the center. On their flanks, the Balearic slingers and Iberian swordsmen readied themselves. The Numidian cavalry, with their swift horses, gathered on the wings, while the war elephants were the lead position.

When the battle commenced, the Carthaginian forces charged with a ferocity that shook the earth. Surus, with Titus and Cleopatra at her side as usual, plowed through the Roman lines, creating a path for the infantry to follow. Syrian archers, positioned behind the elephants, unleashed volleys of arrows that fell on the Romans like deadly rain.

Cleopatra's skill as an archer was well known, even here because the Romans had spread her fame as an immortal Amazon queen throughout the Roman dominions. Encouraging the myth proved to be a beneficial psychological warfare tactic for when Roman soldiers saw her pulling the bowstring fear ran rampant in their ranks.

The battle raged on and the Romans, disciplined and unyielding, pushed back. Surus, amidst all the chaos, suffered another grievous wound in her chest. Titus, seeing his companion in pain, knew that the tide was turning against them. He made a silent vow to protect Surus, no matter the cost.

As night fell the Carthaginian forces were forced to retreat. Hasdrubal the Bald was mortally wounded. The Romans captured and executed him. Behemoth disappeared mysteriously. Titus and Cleopatra found themselves among the few survivors. They shared a common goal: to return Surus to Carthage across the treacherous waters of the Mediterranean. It was a daunting task, for the Roman navy patrolled the seas, and the journey would be fraught with danger.

The survivors took refuge in the walled city of Cornus, where their Sardinian allies held off the Romans long enough for them to make it aboard the remnants of the fleet. Initially, some objected to bringing Surus, but there were enough veterans who had fought for Hannibal and had witnessed her bravery that they convinced the others to let her board one of the ships. Under the darkness of a moonless sky the fleet of five ships set sail for Carthage.

The sea was calm, and the small fleet slipped through the Roman blockade. The journey was long, and the threat of discovery loomed over them like a specter. But fortune favored them.

Titus tended to Surus' wounds as she lay on the deck of the ship. Dirt and straw had been spread to make her more comfortable.

"You never complain," Titus said to her as he rubbed a poultice of herbs and mud into her broken tusk. "You are the bravest elephant in the world."

Cleopatra came up on deck from below with a terracotta jug of water and soothing herbs. She placed it where Surus could reach it with her trunk, but the elephant ignored it. She seemed listless as she gazed out to sea. The gentle rocking of the ship caused her to sleep for several hours.

"Her wounds will heal but she is acting strange," she said. "Is there no way to get her to drink? It would make her feel better, I think."

"I think she may miss Behemoth," he said. "They were good friends."

"More than friends," she said.

"More than friends?"

"He was interested in her."

He looked puzzled. Then they were startled when Surus suddenly stood up. They stepped back to give her room as she stretched her body and lowered her hind quarters.

“This is not something she has done before,” he said.

Cleopatra grinned and looked at him. “You’re going to be a father.”

He looked even more puzzled at her, then stared at Surus. “How can that be?”

“Those long, cold nights when they were alone, perhaps,” she said, smiling.

“You are full of surprises,” he said to Surus. “Aren’t you a little old?

Surus looked back at them, her eyes moist as she steadied herself on the deck. She would settle down again, then stand repeatedly for the next two days. Titus and Cleopatra were soon joined by the crew in the vigil.

“Something’s happening,” a sailor said, waking them up on the third morning.

They came over to her and Titus stroked her trunk. “How are you doing, old girl?” he asked. She answered with her soothing throat rumble.

“She is close,” Cleopatra said.

“How do you know?”

“It’s a female thing.”

“Oh,” was all he could say.

They turned back to Surus at the sound of her expelling a long breath followed by rapid, short breaths as she arched her back and lowered her hind quarters in a squat. Then she slowly expelled the amniotic sac. They could see the calf's head inside. She pushed again and the sac dropped to the deck and burst, releasing the amniotic fluid and calf. She straightened up and turned around to see her calf. With her help, and a little from Titus and Cleopatra, the male calf was standing on wobbly legs and searching for its first meal from his mother.

The ship's crew cheered as the calf nuzzled under Surus. Titus beamed as if he was the proud father. Cleopatra leaned against him, and he drew her close.

The smallest and fastest of the ships sped ahead of the fleet to reach Carthage a day before its arrival. By the time the fleet pulled into the harbor thousands stood on the wharf to greet them as heroes, no matter that they had been defeated. News of the war was sparce and they welcomed the survivors home not only as treasured citizens but for the news they brought on the fates of their loved ones. After generations of war, they may have been accustomed to great loss, but it never got easy hearing that a husband, son, brother, uncle, or nephew would never return.

Remarkably, they had received news from time to time on the exploits of Titus, his magnificent elephant Surus, and now his wife and fellow warrior Cleopatra. They cheered wildly as the three came down the gangplank to the wharf. Then the crew broke out in laughter and applause as the newest member of the clan followed his mother down the gangplank.

He was small and filled with exuberance, and he already had a name that it would take some doing to live up to—Behemoth.

Epilogue

Titus and Cleopatra would become pillars of the community as their family grew to include four children, three sons and a daughter. As with veterans of all wars, Titus and Surus returned to working in the forests while Cleopatra made a home for him and the children. Lucius had died while Titus was in Italia, but his mother and sisters were well. The sisters had married and had families of their own. His mother lived with the oldest.

Titus and Surus would have many adventures, and Behemoth would join them as he grew to an immense size. Then one day in the year 202 BC, a message came from Hannibal.

The year before, the war had shifted from Hispania and Italia to Naraggara, just twenty miles from the city of Carthage when Hannibal old nemesis Publius Cornelius Scipio led twenty-thousand Roman soldiers to invade the country.

Hannibal, along with generals Hasdrubal Gisco, who also fought the Romans in Hispania, and Syphax, the king of the Masaesyli tribe of western Numidia who had switched sides from supporting Rome to Carthage, gathered thirty-thousand infantry and six thousand cavalry to defend the homeland.

Titus and Surus arrived in time to join eighty other war elephants and to take part in the last fight Hannibal would lead, later to become known as the Battle of Zama that resulted in a decisive Roman victory primarily due to the Roman cavalry's superior training.

By this time, the Romans had perfected their tactics to defeat the war elephants. History does not record how many, if any, survived. Over twenty-thousand Carthaginians were killed and as many were captured. With no standing army left, the country was forced to accept Rome's harsh peace treaty, stripping it of all overseas territories and having to pay the heavy war indemnity of ten thousand talents (over $142 million in today's dollars) to be paid over a fifty-five-year period.

Hannibal became a politician but pressure from Rome and political opponents forced him to leave the country. For a time, he served in the court of King Antiochus III of Syria, where he acted as an advisory and sometime mercenary in continuing his fight against Rome. It was at about this time that Titus and Cleopatra migrated back to her hometown in Syria. In addition to their four children, they brought Surus and Behemoth with them.

They were sad to say goodbye to their former general, friend and patron-grandfather to their children when he was forced to go on the run when Roman mercenaries came hunting for him. He traveled alone from country to country trying to make a living in the only trade he knew as a military leader.

His last advisory position and refuge was with King Prusias of Bithynia. When the mercenaries showed up demanding the king turn him over to them, Hannibal went into the countryside and lived a solitary life for a few months in a small stone building. Then one day in 183 BC as the mercenaries surrounded the building and demanded he come out; he ended his life on his own terms by taking poison.

He joined his brothers in history as having lost the war that led to the Roman Empire becoming the dominate power in the Mediterranean for centuries. Hasdrubal died before him at the Battle of Metaurus in 207 BC. Mago fought throughout the Italia campaign and in the Balearic Island. He received orders to join Hannibal in Carthage but after being severely wounded in Italia he died at sea. Hannibal's nephew Hanno, who often led the Numidian cavalry, disappeared from history after 215 BC when he captured Crotona, in southern Italia.

Rome's long memory, though, caused it to return to Carthage a full one hundred thirty-eight years later in what would become known as the Third Punic War when it would obliterate the entire nation, killing nearly every citizen and leveling the cities. Those who were not killed fled or were sold into slavery and Carthage ceased to exist.

About the author

John Chadwell is the author of eight other novels, including: *Werewolves of New Idria: Holy Warriors, Hunt of the Sea Wolves, Pershing – The Soldiers' General, Major Crime Unit: Operation Casablanca, The Kid and Wild Bill, Ghost of the U-85, Last Sunrise,* and *Legends and Liars*. John wrote two screenplays that were produced: *God's Club* and *Midnight Movie Massacre*. He is a 20-year Navy veteran serving as a photojournalist, and worked for over 30 years as a freelance reporter. He lives in Northern California with his wife, Diane.

Other publications by John Chadwell

Short Stories

Charlie Butterfield

Letter from a Soldier

Screenplays

Werewolves of New Idria